THUNDER ROAD

BADLANDS BOOK 7

MORGAN BRICE

eBook ISBN: 978-1-64795-086-6
Print ISBN: 978-1-64795-087-3

Darkwind Press is an imprint of DreamSpinner Communications, LLC

THUNDER ROAD

BADLANDS BOOK 7

By Morgan Brice

1

SIMON

"You look lost." Simon glanced up as he unpacked from their honeymoon. Vic stood in the bedroom doorway of their blue bungalow.

Vic shook his head to clear his zoned-out expression and smiled. "Not lost. Just a little surprised."

Simon tossed a shirt into the laundry basket. "About what?"

Vic shrugged. "I guess I thought being married would feel different somehow."

Simon cocked his head and gave him a look. "What, like the ghost of Freddie Mercury would show up and sing 'Crazy Little Thing Called Love'?"

Vic laughed. "Not exactly, although I wouldn't turn down 'We Will Rock You.'" He did the signature stomp rhythm and Simon chuckled.

Simon came around to Vic's side of the bed. "Seriously—like what?"

Vic looked away, blushing. "Never mind. It's silly."

Simon touched Vic's chin with his forefinger and lifted his face. "Not silly. Tell me."

Vic sighed. "I honestly don't know. More earth-shaking, somehow?"

"I thought we shook the earth pretty well last night," Simon replied with a sexy tone that made Vic redden even more.

"Yes, we did. But I meant the everyday stuff feeling changed, I guess. And it's just like normal—only with rings."

Simon took Vic into his arms, enjoying the height difference of his husband being a few inches taller. "We've been living together for a while now. I think that was the big adjustment. Now we're just us again, but with a spiffy certificate and some new jewelry. Didn't even change names."

"Kincaide-D'Amato or D'Amato-Kincaide doesn't really fall trippingly off the tongue," Vic replied.

"Dunno. You've got a very talented tongue." Simon leaned in for a kiss, deepening it from a press of lips to demonstrate his point.

"I don't know what I expected," Vic said when they separated. "That's why I said it was silly. It's a big thing to be able to get married. And I loved our wedding and the reception and honeymoon. But I'm still me, and you're still you, and we're still us, if that makes any sense."

Simon dove in for another quick kiss. "Yes, in a weird way. I think I know what you mean. And you're right—we did the whole adjustment over what drawers to use and how to navigate sharing the bathroom and kitchen when you moved in. So while getting married was a big emotional and legal milestone, we had already done the adjusting."

"It was all wonderful, and everything passed in a blur," Vic replied. "The bachelor parties, the wedding, the honeymoon all absolutely perfect. But it was a whirlwind. Now we're back to normal, and I'm trying to sync up, I guess."

Simon laughed. "That's as good a way to put it as any. Nothing's changed—but everything changed."

Their friends and families had given them the best bachelor parties Simon ever imagined, followed by the wedding of their dreams. They honeymooned at a haunted castle in England, which was memorable for many reasons, both personal and paranormal.

Now that they were home, the past few months seemed like a fantasy.

"I imagine it was a lot different back when people didn't live together first and waited to have sex," Vic added.

Simon snorted. "Yeah, like that was going to happen."

"I'm just sayin'," Vic protested with a naughty grin. "Theoretically."

They had been living together for a while, realizing soon after they got together that this relationship wasn't like anything either of them experienced before. The connection between them was electric, overcoming Vic's hesitance about the supernatural and Simon's initial skepticism regarding law enforcement. To Simon's eye, that proved they were meant to be.

Simon owned Grand Strand Ghost Tours on the Myrtle Beach boardwalk, where he used his psychic abilities to provide readings and seances. His ghost tours were popular because he knew the history and lore around Myrtle Beach's famous haunts and often got insights from the ghosts themselves.

All the paranormal "woo-woo" had been difficult for Vic to accept at first. He was a down-to-earth Pittsburgh homicide detective who had relocated to the shore. His job depended on facts and evidence, and it had taken a while for Vic to accept that Simon's gifts were real.

Since then, Simon often worked as an official consulting expert for the Myrtle Beach Police Department. Simon and Vic, with his partner Ross Hamilton, had solved a notable number of cases and stopped human and supernatural threats. It had taken work to develop their professional partnership, but now both the work and off-duty sides of their lives were finally in sync.

"For the amount of time we spent naked, we sure have a lot of dirty laundry," Simon observed, looking at the overflowing basket. "How did that happen?"

"It was too chilly to go out without clothing, and we didn't want to get arrested." Vic tossed another pair of socks into the pile.

"Have you heard from Ross? Did the department survive without you? No crime sprees?"

Vic rolled his eyes. "Myrtle Beach isn't exactly known for its crime waves, but apparently, things stayed pretty quiet. Ross hasn't given me a lot of details—said he'd fill me in when I went to the station. I think he's doing his best to help me extend that honeymoon feeling as long as possible."

"Yeah, Pete keeps telling me that nothing much happened with the store." Simon closed his empty suitcase and zipped it shut. "I mostly believe him, and I appreciate that he handled everything well on his own. But I guess we had to return to the real world sooner or later."

As much as Simon had enjoyed the time away with Vic, he also liked running Grand Strand Ghost Tours and enjoyed helping people—living and dead—with his psychic abilities. He knew the value of being able to provide answers and closure, and his insights had brought killers to justice and solved cold cases, helping the spirits rest in peace.

"Of course, we're getting back just in time for the craziness that happens in the fall." Vic set his empty suitcase aside. "I'm not sure I'm ready for *that*, but it is what it is. Motorcycle season is starting. That's always busy—for good reasons and bad."

Myrtle Beach had been a favorite destination for motorcyclists and cycle clubs practically since the bikes were invented. Road rallies ended in town with celebrations on the Boardwalk. Cycle clubs held fall gatherings once the beaches weren't quite as crowded and the temperatures were more leather-friendly. Local cops cracked down on cars and cyclists cruising Ocean Boulevard, but people managed to make several passes before being shooed away and then returned.

Bikes and bikers were a subject of conversation. Businesses appreciated the influx of visitors in the shoulder season—the months when the weather was warm, but most of the tourists had gone home. It picked up some of the slack from the exodus of beachgoers. Locals grumbled about traffic and noise, and some held outdated impressions that raised questions about crime or violence.

As Vic frequently pointed out, thanks to how expensive good bikes had become, the average bike owner was forty-seven. Which was at odds with the perception of young toughs from fifties-era movies.

Not that carousing didn't happen, but the average rider was also married and much more likely to be an accountant or a doctor than a drifter.

"It's usually not the bikers causing the problems," Vic said. "It's the people who come to the bars to hang out and pretend. They've seen *Roadhouse* a few too many times and want to live the dream." That usually meant they woke up hungover and needing bail.

"In some ways, I like the summer drunks better than the fall drunks," Vic went on. "The summer drunks are younger and happier. They're still in college, so they're used to getting blitzed and then going to class. The Halloween crowd is older, and they're trying to relive their glory days, but they've lost the knack. I hate getting pulled into rounding them up."

As a homicide detective, busting drunks wasn't usually part of Vic's regular job. But when things got out of hand, he ended up pitching in. "You've got it easy. At least dead people don't throw up on your shoes."

"Look at the bright side. We'll go to a party, and it'll be fine— like it always is," Simon said with a smile, knowing how to smooth his husband's ruffled feathers.

Vic kissed him. "I forget that this is your busy season too."

"I'm booked pretty solid," Simon agreed. "But that's good because the shop slows down over the holidays—and the people who come in then are not as happy."

Clients who sought out dead loved ones for Halloween tended to have a sense of humor about the whole thing. Around Thanksgiving and Christmas, the messages were sadder as people hoped to contact departed family members.

His work as a medium often had a healing component, helping the bereaved move on and giving the dead peace. Unlike the Halloween thrill-seekers, the customers who sought his services the rest of the year usually needed answers or sought absolution. Simon saw his abilities as far more than a boardwalk diversion.

"Don't work too hard," Vic teased. "We've still got some honeymoon energy to burn off."

Simon pulled him close and gave him a deep kiss, letting one hand slip down to squeeze Vic's ass while the other teased at his package. "Hold that thought. I promise I won't be too tired."

Vic headed to the precinct while Simon walked to the shop, enjoying a cool morning and the ocean breeze. He sipped coffee from a travel mug and lifted his face to the salt air, appreciating a moment of calm.

Intuition told him things were about to get more exciting before winter set in.

Simon had learned to love shoulder season. Some businesses closed over the winter, while others were open for shorter hours. The beach wasn't deserted, but the boardwalk and restaurants weren't jammed like in the summer. The city's rhythms were the opposite of his old life, and Simon didn't miss the past at all.

Several years ago, Dr. Sebastian Simon Kincaide taught Folklore and Mythology at a college in Columbia, South Carolina, where he had grown up in a wealthy family. Then a student's very religious parent had accused him of teaching Satanism, the college had caved under pressure, and Simon lost his professorship, and soon after, his fiancé left him.

Angry and needing a new start, Simon found his way to Myrtle Beach after an aunt offered him the use of her bungalow. When she and his uncle retired to Florida, they sold him the house and wished him well.

He'd met Vic when the skeptical detective had been stymied by a serial killer and was desperate enough to ask a psychic for help. They had solved the case, sparks flew, and he and Vic ended up together.

"Hey, boss! How's it going?" Pete King, Grand Strand Ghost Tours' assistant store manager, greeted Simon when he walked in.

"Not too bad, but the day's still young. Any new requests for bookings?"

"You're nearly booked solid for October," Pete said. "At least, as solid as you want to be. I think I could fill every slot if you wanted."

"I'd be among the dead by Halloween if I did that." Simon leaned against the counter. "And I have a husband to consider now."

Contacting the spirits drained energy, and the longer the connection or the more difficult the spirit was to reach, the faster the medium was depleted. Simon had learned the hard way to manage his gift so that he didn't end up flat on his back or so tired that it took days to recover.

Pete grinned. "How's Vic adapting to married life?"

"We're both finding it's not quite as different as we expected." Simon finished his coffee and set the insulated cup aside. "At least so far."

"I'm the wrong person to know," Pete said. "Still footloose and fancy-free."

"Don't let Mikki hear you say that."

"Mikki's the one who's allergic to weddings. I'm working on him."

Pete stayed up front while Simon went to the office and checked his schedule. He had several readings for customers in the morning, a meeting at the Grand Strand Sculpture Gardens after lunch to discuss a Halloween event, and a reminder to leave early for dinner with Vic.

"We got a call from a guy named Carter Edwards, the president of one of the motorcycle clubs," Pete said from the doorway. "He wants you to contact some of their members who have passed away."

"Accidents? Unusual circumstances?"

"He didn't say," Pete replied. "But he seemed really nervous. Like it was a big deal to him."

"Fine. Go ahead and set something up. I'm intrigued." Few things involving the dead constituted a true emergency that couldn't wait. Simon had a hunch that the request was more than it seemed, and he had learned to go with his intuition.

"He asked to talk to you as soon as possible. You have an open spot marked 'office' this morning—can you meet with him then?" Pete asked.

"Yeah. This time. Don't want to make a habit of it."

"I'll let him know," Pete said.

"Did you get the name of the club?"

Pete handed him a sheet from the phone notepad. "They're the Low Rangers. I looked them up—his number and the club website are on the paper. Already did a little checking. From what I found, back in the eighties they were quite a wild bunch—got in trouble with the law, raised some hell, were the bad boys of the Grand Strand.

"Then they went straight, after some of their members died in rumbles or went to prison," Pete went on. "Now they do charity fundraisers, holiday food bank drives, help out at senior centers, and volunteer to rehabilitate rescue dogs. Vic could probably tell you more."

Simon thought through what Pete said because his sixth sense pinged. "So the members cleaned up their act and do a lot of things that could be viewed as absolution," he mused. "When you said members died, was that in fights with other clubs, accidents, cops, or what?"

Pete leaned against the counter. "It depends on who wrote the story. All of those have been mentioned, especially in the early days. But one article claimed that the Low Rangers allegedly made a deal with *something* back in the day to save the club members from dying in a gang war. The price has been one life a year ever since."

Simon raised his eyebrows. "One life a year? For how long?"

"Since the eighties," Pete replied. "So of course I had to verify, and I found a list of names and dates. They all check out as being real people, real club members, and really dead—or rather missing and presumed dead."

"Cause of death?"

"Vanished without a trace; never seen again." Pete shot him a self-satisfied smile at his research skills. "Sounds like a bad bargain to me."

Simon caught his breath. "That matches a lot of dangerous stories. Demon deal, Wild Hunt."

"Those came to mind."

"Forty-some people gone missing? Maybe dead. Why does

anyone join the club? Why don't they all quit?" Simon's mind reeled.

"The Low Rangers draw from cyclists with a rough past," Pete said. "They've always been a criminal gang—except now they're reformed outlaws. All of them have done jail time. They aren't choir boys, but they're also not looking for trouble anymore. I guess people join to make up for their past. The legends say that the peace arrangement forged by the Rangers is why there hasn't been a gang war since then in Myrtle Beach."

"It makes sense," Simon replied. "And I could see the club as welcoming. Back in the day, there were monasteries that offered a chance to do good work within a community that would maintain accountability. People could contribute without being out in the larger world by making wine, copying manuscripts, that sort of thing."

"Not as many options now," Pete agreed. "And there's a fatalistic romance to taking your chances over being the next sacrifice for a good cause, especially if you don't think your life is worth much otherwise."

Simon believed the club members' lives had value, but he understood why someone who had a lifelong run of bad circumstances could conclude otherwise.

"Well, you've got me hooked. I wonder what Vic's heard about the club."

"When you find out, let me know," Pete said. "This is right before the Myrtle Beach Monster Motorcycle Mania rally. Coincidence?"

"Shit. I managed to forget about that. It's the season, right?"

Pete nodded. "As soon as the back-to-school stuff goes on clearance, it's spooky time."

Simon had mixed feelings about Halloween. As a kid, he loved the costumes and candy. As a folklore professor, the cultural celebration fascinated him. And as a medium, sometimes the press of spirits at a time when the Veil was thin seemed overwhelming.

He and Vic decorated the bungalow and gave out candy for

Trick-or-Treat, and they usually got invited to someone's Halloween party or went to a shindig at a favorite bar.

But those with abilities remained watchful. After the autumn solstice, the balance favored darkness over light until spring. And while most people gave little notice to anything except the time change, those who dealt with magic and energy recognized a real, primordial shift.

Simon made sure to renew the wardings on the shop and bungalow, recharge their protective amulets under the light of a full moon, and reconsecrate the sigils and runes that provided a powerful deterrent to dangerous supernatural entities.

Despite all the precautions, Simon relied on his psychic radar and the warnings of helpful ghosts to keep the darkness at bay.

"Has Vic finally adjusted to the ghost stuff?" Pete asked. It was a fair question, given how skeptical Vic had been when they first met.

"Mostly. He doesn't doubt that it's all true, and he believes my abilities are real. He knows more about what goes bump in the night than he used to. Honestly—Vic sees enough darkness with what the living can do that I'm just as glad he doesn't know all the dangers from the other side."

Simon went to get another cup of coffee and sat at the breakroom table to take a few minutes to get ready for Edwards. He closed his eyes, stilled his thoughts, and focused on his breathing. Ghosts with something to say could usually get his attention even when his mind was busy; tuning in was easier when he silenced the internal chatter.

He had never given the motorcycle rally much consideration other than when it bogged down traffic or the roar of the engines made it hard to think. Vic rode a black Hayabusa and sometimes enticed Simon to ride behind him, but he never felt completely comfortable on the bike.

Vic, on the other hand, loved to ride but viewed the clubs with skepticism. Most were just enthusiasts having fun, but a few left a wake of vandalism and public nuisance complaints behind them, a mess for the cops to handle.

In the ether, Simon sensed the low hum of spirits gathering.

Even non-believers and those without a whiff of paranormal ability could pick up on the shift, which gave rise to the season's stories.

Pete poked his head into the room. "Mr. Edwards is here. He's at the front counter."

Simon released his meditation, thanking the energies and invoking their protection. Any time mortals interacted with the other realms of existence, there was risk. Simon knew that all too well from readings that went dangerously wrong.

Just in case, he kept an emergency flask of salted holy water laced with colloidal silver and iron filings, a mixture likely to repel most supernatural creatures.

Simon walked up front and saw a man with long gray hair waiting at the counter. The visitor wore a leather motorcycle vest over black jeans and boots and looked the part of a bad boy biker.

"Mr. Edwards? I'm Simon Kincaide," he greeted his client, concentrating on learning everything he could from their initial contact.

Edwards looked to be in his late fifties or early sixties, and the lines around his eyes and sun damage to his face suggested those were hard years. He had a trim build, still solid. One hand rested on the counter, and Simon saw old broken knuckles that hadn't healed right.

A hint of darkness clung to the man like a geas—or perhaps, Simon thought, it was the weight of a bad bargain made more than half a century ago.

Edwards extended his hand, and Simon shook it, picking up more psychic information. *He's not just nervous—he's scared.*

"Please, have a seat." Simon ushered him to the table he used for readings in the shop's alcove, separated from the main area by a curtain.

Edwards sat, and Simon took the seat across from him. The man smelled faintly of old sweat, cheap aftershave, and worn leather.

"I want to make a trade," Edwards blurted before Simon could ask any questions. "I want them to take me this year and I don't know how to let them know."

Simon was grateful for the research Pete had done because otherwise the man's outburst would have made no sense. He suspected that he knew what Edwards meant, but he needed to be sure.

"I don't think I follow. I'll be more help if you can please start at the beginning."

Edwards looked around nervously as if he was afraid of being overheard.

"Don't worry. Pete will make sure we're not disturbed, and you can count on his discretion," Simon assured his guest. "How can I help you?"

"A long time ago, my club made a bargain to stop something bad from happening," Edwards said. "We agreed to pay a powerful third party in exchange for keeping the peace. For forty years, that maintained a truce that saved a lot of lives."

"You want to change the bargain?" Simon knew from folklore that such things never went well.

"No!" Edwards looked frightened, as if they might be over-heard. "Every year, to keep the peace, someone from our club goes to…join…the third party. They pick someone according to their own measures. I don't know who they intend to choose this year, but I want them to take me."

Simon's intuition picked up a powerful mix of feelings—sadness, regret, and resignation.

"Why do you want to be taken?" Simon noticed that Edwards didn't clarify what was involved in the taking or who the third party was, but it tracked with what Pete had uncovered.

"I've been with the club for forty years," Edwards said. "They're more my family than anyone who's blood kin to me. We've been through a lot together. They're my brothers, sons—hell, grandsons. I haven't lived a good life, and it's catching up to me."

He paused for a deep, wracking cough, and Simon read *emphy-sema* from his thoughts as if the sound left room for doubts.

"All those cigs I smoked finally caught up to me." Edwards gave a bitter smile. "Then again, I never thought I'd live long enough for it to matter. James Dean didn't."

He paused to cough again, and it took longer for him to catch his breath. "Fucking COPD. Doc says I don't have much time left. That's why it should be me. Got nothing to lose."

Simon read the sincerity in the man's voice. "You don't know how they choose who to take?"

He wanted to ask who "they" were. Such deals could rarely be broken, but sometimes alternate bargains could be struck depending on what the entity valued.

Edwards shook his head. "I've watched it happen all these years, heard plenty of talk. All anyone is sure of is that it's one person, once a year, to stop the bad things, to keep the peace and all the other members safe."

If that's the deal Edwards's long-ago club president made with an entity, the man was an idiot, Simon thought. Creatures like the fay or demons were the origin of the phrase "the devil's in the details." Both were more meticulous than any lawyer, with centuries of experience in deception.

Simon didn't want to believe the bargain was quite that awful, but it wouldn't be the first time a clueless mortal got led astray by a smooth-talking supernatural creature.

"Do you know any details about where the original deal was made?" Simon asked. "Location, date, any special ceremony or offering?"

This didn't sound like a crossroads deal, not that demons wouldn't welcome a steady tribute of souls. It had all the earmarks of something fey, which was much worse.

"That's where I was hoping you could help." Edwards licked his lips nervously. "I don't know if the ones who were taken died, but I assume they did. Can you contact them?"

If this was, as Simon feared, a deal with the fay or a similarly ancient creature, there was no way to guess their willingness to make a trade. Some might find human sentiment amusing and do so out of ennui. Others were legalistic in the extreme and likely to take offense.

"Who do you want to contact in the afterlife?" Simon believed Edwards was sincere, and he appreciated the man's willingness to offer himself to save someone who might have more years ahead of them.

"Dennis disappeared last year. Michael the year before that. Rodney and then Aaron. Can we start with them?"

Simon put his hands out, palms up, and Edwards's cold fingers gripped him. "Close your eyes. There are spirits near, but I'm not sure whose." Simon focused inwardly on the ghosts he sensed were close. They weren't visible, but they were definitely tangible.

"Dennis. Rodney. Michael. Aaron. Your friend Carter Edwards is here, and he would like to speak with you." Simon spoke into the ether and waited for a response.

He could feel the spirits' agitation but wasn't sure of the reason. *Is something keeping them from answering, or don't they want to respond?*

One of the ghosts ventured closer. "Carter—is that you?" Simon relayed what the spirits said, supplying as much detail as he could.

"Denny? Yes, I'm here. God, Denny. Are you dead?" Despite his tough appearance, Edward's voice broke.

"Yeah, Carter. That was the deal. They took us, and we died. All of us."

In Simon's mind, he saw Denny as a wiry man in his forties who looked like he had seen hard times. Close behind him were three others, all equally rough-looking, still clad in biker leathers.

Edwards choked back a sob. "I'm sorry. I've missed you."

"It was time, bro," one of the other ghosts, a large, broad-chested man, replied. "Wasn't gonna live forever, and my number should have been up long ago."

"Are you okay?" Edwards's voice shook.

"Could be worse," a third spirit replied, this one older than the rest with graying temples. "I'm not downstairs. Wasn't counting on upstairs. Better than I deserve."

"You don't look good, Carter," the fourth ghost said. "Gonna be heading our way soon."

Edwards gripped Simon's hands tightly. "That's why I called you. I don't have long, and someone else can get a little more time." He paused, and when he spoke again, his voice was steady. "I thought you might know how I can find the one we made the deal with and ask him to take me next."

Simon heard the murmur of distant voices as the ghosts conferred among themselves. "We fade here," one of the spirits replied. "It feeds."

A shudder went through Edwards, and Simon didn't fault his reaction.

"They screwed up when they made the deal," Edwards said. "Didn't mind the details."

"We're not much for lawyers," the first ghost said, and their laughter chilled Simon.

"Can I do it? Can I get a message through to the dealmaker? Can you ask him?" Edwards pressed.

Simon felt the ghosts tire and knew he couldn't keep the connection much longer.

"We'll pass it along," the third spirit replied. "No promises."

"Thank you." Edwards slumped with relief. "See you soon."

Simon felt the four ghosts depart, but another presence lingered at the edge of his perception. It wasn't human, but it was definitely interested, although it made no move to get closer.

"Who are you?" Simon asked silently.

"He called, and I answered," the entity replied.

"You're the dealmaker?"

"I have been many things."

"Did you hear his request?" Simon sensed that whatever creature had answered the call was powerful and ancient, and probably never human.

"I did. I will consider it. The time has come to take another offering."

Courtesy when dealing with immortal spirits was essential for self-preservation, something Simon took seriously, but the lore was clear that thanking the fay could imply an unwanted indebtedness.

The ghosts and entity vanished from Simon's Sight, leaving him drained. Edwards gasped, and Simon held up a hand to keep Pete from coming closer.

"Stay back. I haven't opened the wardings yet."

Simon spoke the incantation to cleanse the space and dispel

ghosts and any other powers attracted by the séance. He dismissed the call to the spirits and thanked the ghosts, making sure to strengthen the protections in case the entity thought about coming back. Simon wasn't sure what Edwards and his club had summoned, but Simon hoped he never dealt with it again.

He sensed when the energies cleared and felt relieved when Edwards straightened his shoulders.

"Thank you." Edwards let go of Simon's grip. "That's as much as I can ask for."

"You know that the entity is feeding on the ghosts." Simon felt the need to make that point clear.

"I'm not surprised. We don't call it that in the club, but on some level, I think we all know. Maybe it'll take me next. Maybe it won't. But at least I tried—and I got to hear from my boys again."

Edwards's craggy features softened a bit, looking less agitated. Whatever crimes he had committed and however he had paid for them, the biker seemed at peace. "Helluva thing you can do, raising ghosts like that. I wasn't sure you were the real deal when I walked in, but you've got what my grandma called the shine."

"You're welcome," Simon replied. "Go in peace."

Edwards paid for the session. Simon and Pete watched him leave.

"What did you make of that?" Pete asked.

"How much did you hear?"

"Pretty much all of it."

Simon shook his head. "I wish I knew what they conjured. It was a fairly powerful entity. This is why casting magic when you don't know what you're doing is a bad thing."

"Think it'll give him what he wants?"

"No way to know." Simon shrugged. "Depends on how much it enjoys jerking mortals around."

Simon cleansed the energies around his work table again and said another blessing, just in case. Pete ducked into the break room and returned with a chocolate bar and a cup of coffee.

"Eat. Drink. You need it after that." Pete pushed the items into his hands. "I'll smudge and replace the protections."

Now that the séance was over, Simon felt drained, tired enough he thought he might fall asleep in his chair. After channeling spirits for years, he wasn't surprised, recognizing the cost of connecting to the other side. Food, drink, and sleep would replace what he had spent.

Fortunately, the rest of the afternoon passed quietly. Simon went into his office to work on bookkeeping while Pete handled the few customers who wandered in.

Just before sunset, as they were closing for the night, Vic called.

"Hey, I'm going to be late for dinner. All the uniforms got called out to an accident, and I said I'd help cover until some of them came back."

"What happened?" A cold premonition slithered through Simon's bones.

"Don't know the details, but a guy on a Harley hit a car, and from what the witnesses are saying, he just disappeared," Vic recounted. "They can't all be drunk."

Simon managed a sad smile. "Older guy, biker leathers?"

Vic hesitated. "Yeah. How did you know?"

"It's a long story. I just did a séance for him. Seems like someone was listening. You can look for the body all you want, but you're not going to find it."

2

VIC

"Want to run that by me again?" Vic did his best not to go into what Simon called cop mode over the phone. "We've got his bike, but no body. Where the hell did he go?"

"Short answer—something like the fay took him to pay this year's tribute for a deal made forty years ago to avert a gang war," Simon replied.

Vic was quiet for a moment, reminding himself that Simon was his husband and not a random witness. "I don't understand."

Simon sighed. "Check your records. A member of the bike club, the Low Rangers, has gone missing every year for forty years. None of them were ever found. I can have Pete send you the research he did before I conducted the séance. Carter Edwards is now the most recent addition."

Vic knew Edwards's name from the motorcycle registration, and he guessed the club membership from the stickers on what was left of the bike. Simon got it right on both counts.

"When did you see Edwards?"

"I squeezed him in for my first appointment. He was here for about an hour, and then he left."

Vic pinched the bridge of his nose. "And Edwards was dead—or gone—by noon."

"Fuck," Simon muttered.

Ross gave him a questioning look, overhearing Vic's side of the conversation, and Vic mouthed, "later."

"Yeah. No blood, no body, no squishy bits. Like no one had been riding the bike, except witnesses all described the same man from moments before the crash."

"How is that going over?"

"About as well as you'd expect." Vic took a swig of his coffee and wished he was off duty to have a shot of something stronger. "This is South Carolina. Half the population is going to blame the Rapture, and the other half is going to think it's a secret government death ray."

"Do you want me to come down there and make a statement?" Simon asked.

Vic sighed. He hated dragging Simon into what might become a high-profile case once the media heard about it, but he didn't see another option. "Yeah. Since you were maybe the last person he talked to."

"If I park in the back and you let me in the staff door, anyone watching might just think I was visiting my husband," Simon suggested. "That keeps the rumor mill from getting ahead of us."

"Sounds like a plan. Do you mind bringing dinner with you? Ross is here too. We're both fine with meatball subs. Make it easy."

"Will do. Give me time to order, and I'll be over." Simon ended the call. Vic looked up to see Ross's questioning expression.

"Simon did a séance with the missing motorcyclist earlier today. He's coming over to give a statement. You'd better sit in on it if there's nothing else going on. It's going to be a strange one," Vic told him.

Half an hour later, Simon showed up with warm subs, cold drinks, and a dozen Hot Now donuts.

"Bless you," Ross told Simon as they unpacked the food in the break room. "I really didn't want dinner from the vending machine —again."

"I had to eat anyhow," Simon replied. "And I wasn't going to cook since Vic wouldn't be home."

They kept the conversation light as they ate, chatting about the weather, the big-name concerts playing locally, and the wind-down to the tourist season. When they finished eating, they moved to the interview room. Simon and Vic took up seats at the table across from each other. Ross sat in a chair in the corner.

"Okay. Tell me what happened." Vic started the recording.

"We got a phone call from Edwards, who wanted a psychic reading as soon as possible," Simon told them. "He didn't say why, but said it was urgent. I fit him in, and then Pete did some background research."

"Do you usually look up your new customers?" Vic asked.

"Not always. For most people, there wouldn't be much to see except their social media. I generally prefer not to have preconceived ideas when I meet someone so I can be open to what I pick up from them in person." Simon seemed to be trying not to use language that might seem too woo-woo to someone reading the notes.

"But you did look up Edwards. Why?"

Vic kept his tone moderate, reminding himself again that Simon wasn't a suspect. The situation felt uncomfortably like the early days in their relationship when he was aggressively skeptical about psychic abilities. Plenty of first-hand experience had changed his mind.

"Something seemed off," Simon replied. "Pete picked up on it before I did because he took the call. Edwards seemed a little panicky. I get clients like that sometimes who want a psychic reading and are really looking for a prediction or advice. Should they accept the job? Is the person they're dating the right one? That sort of thing."

"What was off about Edwards wanting a séance?"

"The urgency. The things people want to say to those who have passed aren't usually time-dependent. They want to apologize or make things right or say goodbye," Simon replied. "Occasionally, a client wants to know where the deceased hid the life insurance policies or extra cash, or they need some detail for important paper-work. But that's as urgent as it gets."

"Did you worry that researching the client's background might color the information you provided?" Vic didn't believe that, but he knew someone less familiar with Simon and psychics was bound to ask.

"No. Like I said, it struck Pete as odd, and he had already looked into a lot before he told me about Edwards. We get clients of all ages and walks of life. But in general, hard-core motorcyclists don't stop in often."

"Go on."

"We knew the big rally was coming up—it's fall, so there will be lots of bikes in town. But when Pete looked up the club, he found rumors about the group being cursed. He dug deeper because that sort of thing—if it's true—can make a reading dangerous if I'm not prepared."

"How?" Vic wanted the answers for the record, even though he had worked enough supernatural cases with Simon to understand the process.

"In my world, curses are real. If a witch with real ability has put a root or a hex on a person, I need to know that before I use my abilities. Otherwise, the combination can be bad. Sort of like a supernatural version of mixing bleach and ammonia."

Vic knew Simon was doing his best to explain for any listeners who didn't know much about the paranormal or didn't fully believe it was real. He and Simon had gotten past that point long ago.

Simon twisted his wedding ring, and Vic read the fidgeting to mean his husband was tired and stressed. He knew how much a major spirit reading could take out of Simon, and he likely hadn't had time to rest between then and now.

"Back to the séance. Can you please, for the record, walk us through what happened?"

Simon looked at the microphone. "Normally, I do my best to keep those conversations in confidence, even though I know that provider-client privilege doesn't apply. But since Mr. Edwards is dead and the conversation is directly related, I'm volunteering the information."

Vic nodded encouragingly, and Simon recounted the séance in detail, both the comments by Edwards and the information from the ghosts.

"I can email you the research that Pete and I did so you can follow our sources, but what we found matches what Edwards told us," Simon concluded. "I sensed the entity. It acknowledged the contact but didn't promise anything. Given the accident, it seems like Edwards got what he wanted."

"When you say entity, what sort of creature is powerful enough to make the kind of bargain you're talking about?" Vic asked. He and Simon had gone up against many different paranormal beings in their cases, so he had a few ideas of what might be involved.

"Unlikely to be a ghost," Simon replied. "A powerful witch might be able to lay a curse like that, but the legends that have sprung up around the deaths didn't sound like they were dealing with human magic. The most likely creatures would be a djinn, fay, or demon, but there are many variations of those beings from cultures all around the world.

"By all accounts, the creature kept their side of the bargain. There hasn't been a gang war in Myrtle Beach since the deal was made," Simon went on. "So the bargain didn't just affect the club leader who struck the agreement—it worked a spell that affected the behavior of hundreds of riders over more than half a century. It's very old blood magic."

"Do you think that next year, another club rider will disappear to keep the deal?" Vic asked.

"Yes. Edwards didn't change the deal. He just offered himself as a substitute this year because he was going to die anyhow. The terms didn't require the victim to be young or healthy and left the picking to the entity. So next year, and all the upcoming years, unless someone breaks the curse, someone will die to keep the peace," Simon summarized.

Vic motioned for him to remain silent and turned off the recording.

"Jesus, Mary, and Joseph. That's one hell of a story," Ross said.

"It's not much weirder than the stuff we've already run into," Vic mused. "Just a bigger scale."

"I'm going to ask for help researching this further," Simon told them now that the recorder was off. "We've got friends who are good at figuring out the supernatural side of things. I'd like to know what we're dealing with."

"There's also an interesting dilemma here." Vic leaned back in his chair. "If the club members are told about the risk of joining and the history of deaths and join anyway, embracing the possibility that they could be the next sacrifice, then they are consenting to the danger," Vic said. "People agree to accept the dangers of all kinds of activities, like horseback riding and surfboarding. Sometimes people die doing those things. I'm not sure what authority we have to end the situation—even if we could."

"I thought about that," Simon replied. "And there's also the issue of the truce. Trouble between the motorcycle clubs—especially the less savory ones—happened every year before the deal was made. Club members died—and so did tourists who were in the wrong place at the wrong time. Break the deal, break the truce."

"So the motorcycle club members join knowing they could be sacrificed," Ross said. "The people who would be killed if the clubs start fighting again haven't agreed to the deal."

"Shit." Vic ran his hands through his short, dark hair. "Why does anyone need to die?"

"Because I'm guessing this entity feeds off the death energy. From its perspective, it's gone on a diet by taking one sure meal instead of going feast-or-famine with pure chance," Simon replied. "So the only way to stop the deaths and not start a war—"

"Is to destroy the entity," Vic finished. "Is that even possible?"

Simon shrugged. "Theoretically? Yes. Even gods can die. Look at the Greek myths. But right now, we don't know what this being is, what other powers it has, where its vulnerabilities are—nada. All we know is that one-on-one, with human protections, it's got us way outgunned."

Vic sent Simon home to relax while he and Ross finished the

paperwork. Familiar sounds from the squad room provided a dull hum of ringing phones, humming printers, and the low buzz of conversation. Ross was more quiet than usual, and Vic could sense there was something on his partner's mind.

"Okay, spill. You've got something in your head that's spiraling," Vic said after an hour of seeing Ross fidget.

"That obvious?"

"We've worked together how long? You're not nearly as stealthy as you think," Vic replied.

Ross leaned back and sighed. "Normally we get all kinds of weird stuff around Halloween, but until I started working with you and Simon, I thought it was all just strange people doing bizarre stuff. I always thought Halloween was fun because of that, and I never really understood why some church folks are so set against it."

"And?" Vic suspected he knew where Ross was heading.

"Knowing the kinds of things that you and Simon have dealt with, what's really out there, it's a whole 'nother dimension to the holiday," Ross mused. "Not that I think Trick-or-Treat is of the devil or something. But I wonder if some of the watered-down arguments are rooted in much older, darker legends involving the kinds of creatures that modern people don't think exist."

"Probably." Vic rose to fill his coffee cup again. "People learn to do things the way those who came before them did. But they don't always learn the reason, so over time, the action loses its point."

"I heard a story about a lady who always cut a piece of brisket in half before cooking it because that's how her mother did it. She thought it was something to do with the meat. Turns out her mother had a small pan, and that's the only way the brisket would fit," Ross said with a chuckle.

"Exactly—only in our case, with monsters." Vic deleted another email on his laptop, glad he was nearing the end of his inbox.

"Yeah—still getting used to that," Ross admitted. "The world is a scary place just with *humans*."

"Ain't that the truth," Vic muttered.

"I liked thinking that all the stories about magic and creatures were ways people explained things they didn't understand. Finding out that there's truth underneath the stories is mind-blowing."

"Welcome to my world." Vic glanced at his email when it pinged. "Simon just sent me the information Pete and he compiled on the cycle club. I don't doubt what he told us, but fresh eyes might see something they didn't."

"I did find something interesting," Ross replied. "In the years from 1944 to 1974, there was at least one motorcycle gang war every year in the Carolinas. Anywhere from five to fifteen people ended up dead in each altercation, not to mention tens of thousands of dollars every year in property damage. Also pretty common for bystanders to get hurt too."

"Huh. So five people a year for thirty years might be on the low end, but it's still more than one person a year over forty years," Vic said. "Not counting hurt bystanders, damage, business disruption, and losing tourist traffic."

"We can't turn that loose again, Vic. The bargain the club made is a raw deal, but it's better than what went on before."

Vic rubbed his forehead. "I know. And I'm wondering if the entity is something that has always been here or if it hitched a ride with people who settled here from somewhere else."

"If it's from here and it needs to feed, then there should be a pattern of multiple deaths happening at the same time each year— like plagues, fires, floods, that sort of thing," Ross said. "Except this thing makes people disappear. That's a little harder to cover up than just leaving bodies behind."

"Not really. We can't always account for everyone after a flood or a wildfire. When there's an outbreak, it's going to hit homeless people worse, and no one might notice if they disappear," Vic pointed out.

"If whatever-this-is can summon up fires, floods, and plagues, why is it focusing on motorcycle gang wars?"

Vic stared at his coffee as if it held the answers. "We've gotten better at predicting natural disasters and doing damage control. Better record keeping and more cameras. Gang wars are unpredictable, messy, and involve people who stay off the grid. Gang members are also insular—they don't talk to people outside their groups. Easier to hide the damage."

"Why not other types of gangs? Drug dealers, traffickers, stolen goods?"

Vic thought for a moment. "I'm going to go out on a limb here —Simon's the one who knows about folklore. But those other types of gangs are run-of-the-mill criminals. Motorcycle gangs have a dark romance to them—like armored knights from the wrong side of the tracks."

"Romantic criminals? Really?"

Vic shrugged. "People still talk about Billy the Kid, Bonnie and Clyde, Al Capone in a larger-than-life way. Anti-heroes. Truth was, they were scum, but they had something about them that caught the imagination, and they ended up as legends."

Ross thought for a moment before nodding. "Okay. Not saying I agree with that view, but I know what you mean."

"Except for the rallies, I kinda look forward to fall," Vic admitted. "Not as many tourists and fewer teens and twenties or families with kids—so not as many of the problems that come with them."

"I won't say that retirees and empty-nesters don't throw keggers that get out of hand, but it's a lot less common." Ross chuckled. In the squad room, several people laughed loudly, and Vic guessed someone had shared a funny meme.

"The clubs cause noise, and we have to put patrol units out to remind them not to cruise, but they spend a lot of money, and they mostly mind their manners." Vic finished his coffee, eyed the pot, and weighed having another cup. He set his mug aside and got a sports drink out of his drawer instead.

"The regular cops are probably just as busy as ever, but we usually get a break on the murders once things settle down for the winter. Or maybe it's just locals killing each other instead of visitors," Vic added.

"I'm sure there are statistics on that if you really want to know. And one of our cases takes a lot longer than writing tickets for noise complaints and bad parking," Ross pointed out.

"True." Vic shut down his laptop. "I've finished all the forms I can do tonight. Should be interesting when Cap reads them and hears Simon's testimony."

He didn't doubt that Captain Hargrove would believe them—he had proven himself to be receptive to the idea of supernatural elements when he approved adding Simon as an official consultant. Others in the chain of command weren't as open-minded, so they usually had to figure out how to frame the paranormal issues to avoid problems with city hall, local churches, and the media.

Simon sat on the couch watching a movie when Vic got home. He put the popcorn aside and went to kiss Vic, folding him into a hug.

"Long day, huh?"

"You could say that. We don't have people disappear like that all the time."

"You want some popcorn? I made enough to share."

Vic cracked open two beers and carried them to the couch, sitting down close enough to Simon that they pressed together from knee to hip.

"I need to decompress." Vic noted that the action flick was halfway over, and it was one they had watched many times.

"Want me to start the movie again?" Simon offered.

Vic shook his head. "I think my concentration is shot to hell, so I'm fine with just zoning out a little. Sorry not to be better company."

Simon leaned over to brush his lips across Vic's cheek. "I think you're fine just the way you are."

Vic sipped his beer and watched the familiar movie, glad he didn't have to think hard to follow the story. "We read what you sent us. Makes a great story. Hard to believe it's true but…maybe so."

"I'm going to talk to Father Anne and give Miss Eppie and Mrs. Teller a call." Simon cited three of his best sources for supernatural information. "See what they've heard and what they think might be the best way to handle things. Maybe some poor suckers in the past have tried to kill the entity and been poofed out of existence, so we'll know what to avoid."

"Promise you'll be careful." Vic took Simon's hand. "Don't get poofed."

Simon folded Vic's hands between his own. "I will do my very best not to. I have plenty to stick around for."

Vic knew he was being hypocritical making Simon vow not to take chances. Vic was a cop, and risk went with the badge. Growing up in a law enforcement family, Vic had learned to rationalize the dangers and remain cautious without dwelling on the possibilities.

Their time together had proven that Vic was not as good at dealing with the threat of harm when it came to Simon.

Especially since the supernatural problems that threatened Simon's safety were things Vic couldn't punch or stop with a bullet. Although he often backed up Simon when he and his colleagues worked spells or took on paranormal dangers, Vic always fretted that his lack of magic or psychic abilities meant his protections fell short.

"Quit worrying." Simon looked at him with a smirk. "It doesn't take a mind reader to pick up on what you're thinking. And I feel the same way every time you go out to deal with a police problem."

Vic leaned against Simon's shoulder. "I know. We've talked about it and muddled through before. But it doesn't get easier. Like being deployed—there's always risk."

"That's where it helps that we have such an awesome bunch of friends who can save our asses." Simon rested his cheek on the top of Vic's head. "I'm not going to do anything about the entity or the deal until I know what's involved—and if it isn't worth the downside, we walk away and let things go on the way they have been."

"Promise?"

Simon kissed Vic's hair. "Promise."

Vic turned toward Simon and pulled him in for a kiss, slow and tender. He licked at Simon's lips, slipping inside his mouth. Simon's hands moved across Vic's shoulders, down his back, then back up to the nape of his neck, caressing.

"What do you want?" Simon murmured next to his ear, voice deep and sensual. "What will make you feel better?"

Vic pulled back from the kiss far enough to speak. "You. Maybe just slow tonight."

"We don't have to do anything except touch," Simon assured him, letting his hands rove. "We can snuggle—clothing optional."

"I like that," Vic murmured. "Never thought I'd be playing the too tired to tango card as a newlywed."

Simon kissed him again, and Vic let him take the lead. "There isn't a sex quota."

"Are you sure?" Vic joked tiredly.

"Yep. Positive. That's what weekends are for," Simon assured him. "Although if a hand job would relax you, I'm happy to oblige."

"Sounds just like what the doctor ordered—Dr. Kincaide," Vic teased, using Simon's university title.

"I can make that happen." Simon's hand slipped lower, moving between Vic's legs and stroking over his bulge. Vic spread his thighs wider, knowing his jeans were going to get tight very quickly. He returned the favor, rubbing his palm over Simon's half-hard cock.

"How do you want it?" Simon's voice sounded like whiskey and sin.

"Want it together. Want to feel you," Vic replied, already a little breathless.

Simon worked Vic's belt and then unbuttoned his jeans. Vic hurried to slip them off as Simon pushed down the sweatpants he had changed into while waiting for Vic to come home.

Vic closed his hand over their cocks and bit back a moan. They were both leaking pre-come, but not quite enough to ease the friction of rough palms. Simon reached between the couch cushions for the lube he kept handy and added a daub, slicking their hands.

"Not going to last," Vic warned.

"Didn't expect to. Just want to make you feel good before bedtime." Simon's mouth was so close to Vic's ear that his breath made Vic shiver. "Let go, Vic. Come on. Give it up for me."

The low rumble of Simon's voice and the warmth of his breath on Vic's neck was all it took to push Vic over the edge. Vic gasped and arched, spilling over their joined hands. Simon followed seconds later.

When the aftershocks ended, Simon leaned in to kiss Vic. "Better?"

Vic kissed him back. "Much. I like this married stuff."

"Good. Because you're stuck with me now." Simon reached for the box of tissues and cleaned them.

Vic toyed with the ring on Simon's hand. "I think we already established that."

They weren't quite ready for sleep, so Vic brought more beer back while Simon found another favorite movie to rewatch, one that was a comedy instead of a drama and not monster-focused.

Since they were both half-dressed already they ducked into the bedroom to put on sleep pants and T-shirts, tossing their clothes in the laundry basket and washing.

"Good pick," Vic told Simon when they slouched on the sofa together. "Distracting, but I don't have to pay attention."

They switched on who was the little spoon just like they traded places top and bottom with sex. Tonight, Vic was happy to feel Simon's solid body and strong arms anchoring him.

Vic focused on the rhythm of Simon's heart and the pattern of his breathing. That calmed him and helped him finally release the tension of the day. Knowing that Simon didn't judge him for his reaction helped a lot and was one of the many things he loved about his husband.

The movie was enough of a distraction to short-circuit Vic's spiraling thoughts. He didn't have Simon's psychic talent, but cops depended on instinct and intuition, and Vic's rarely proved him wrong.

Those hunches told Vic they hadn't seen the last of problems with the bikers' entity, even though another sacrifice wasn't due for a year. He knew Simon would canvas his friends in the supernatural community and that they would come up with a plan. But that same intuition warned him that finding a solution was likely to be more dangerous than expected, especially when dealing with a powerful creature who was not going to easily accept losing its guaranteed food source.

He laced their fingers together over his belly. Simon nuzzled against his neck, more interested in cuddling than in the movie.

Let it go, he told himself, drinking in Simon's scent. *If it's been going on for forty years, another few days won't matter. We don't have to solve it on the first try.*

Vic wanted to believe that, but he couldn't shake the sense of urgency that there was more to this case than they knew, and what they hadn't figured out might be the most dangerous part.

"Hey, let's go to bed," Simon nudged him, and Vic realized he had dozed off. The movie was over, and the credits were rolling. "I'll check the locks and meet you in there."

Vic shuffled off, glad to put an end to a very disquieting day. His familiar bedtime routine was a welcome comfort. By the time Simon returned from his late-night rounds, Vic had slipped between the covers, waiting for his lover to join him.

"I'll be right there," Simon promised. "Hold my spot."

"Always." Vic managed not to drift off until Simon climbed into bed and threw an arm over him. They would roll apart before long, too warm to sleep like that, but Vic appreciated the gesture.

"Sweet dreams," Simon whispered. "I'm already planning to give you a very happy morning."

3

SIMON

The next day, Simon looked out on a full room of listeners as he read from his latest book about ghosts at the Grand Strand Sculpture Garden.

"I'll be happy to take questions," Simon said when he finished and looked up at his audience with a smile.

Hands shot up in the air. Simon chose an older woman who was three rows back. "What happens if someone asks for a séance but the ghost won't show up? Why wouldn't the spirit come?"

"Good question," Simon replied. "Sometimes ghosts have faded beyond hearing our request for their presence. Where they go or whether they just become part of the universe is beyond my paygrade. But I also believe that they can simply move out of range. If they retain their personality and consciousness, they have good days and bad days, just like the living. It may be a day when they don't feel like talking. I'd advise respecting that and trying again at another time."

That seemed to satisfy the woman who nodded and smiled her thanks.

The next question came from a college-aged man. "Why do

ghosts hang around? If I could go anywhere for free, I wouldn't camp out in some dingy old attic or basement."

That drew laughs, and Simon couldn't help chuckling as well. "I totally agree. Unfortunately, for reasons we don't completely understand, some ghosts are range-limited to whatever is anchoring them to the world of the living. That could be a house or a cemetery, an object, or the place where they died—somewhere or some item that is deeply significant to them."

"What if you haunted something portable and made a deal with someone to take you places after you died?" the young man persisted.

Simon admired his ingenuity. "There are a lot of legends about whether ghosts can cross running water, like rivers, or bodies of water, like lakes and oceans. Many of the legends contradict each other, so it may depend on other factors, like the strength of the ghost or how close it is to an object of attachment.

"If a particular spirit can't cross bodies of water, then international post-mortem travel would be out," Simon continued, and the audience laughed. "Their range could be limited by not being able to cross rivers since large ones, like the Mississippi, can be difficult to avoid. But there are plenty of stories about ghost ships and haunted ships, so the lore isn't really clear.

"Airplanes, however, can be haunted according to the stories," Simon went on. "In those cases, it was because the plane re-used parts from a wreck, so it's not talking about a carry-on ghost brought by a passenger. I love the question. Thank you!"

He took three more questions before time ran out, but none were as inventive. When his host wrapped up the Q&A session, Simon moved to a table with stacks of his books where he could sell and sign copies—and answer more questions.

One older woman hung back, waiting to be at the end of the signing line. She paid for a book and gave Simon her name. "I want to book a séance with you," Shirley Brighton blurted as if she was nervous about asking. "I need to talk with my uncle. He was the last keeper of the Georgetown Light." Her voice dropped to a near whisper. "I don't think they are keeping the protections up like he used to."

That got Simon's attention. "Protections?" There was no one in line behind her, and his host was busy directing the helpers who were putting the room back in order. "I'm not sure I understand. Isn't that lighthouse protected by the Coast Guard?"

She gave him a mysterious smile. "There's protection and *protection*. The Coast Guard never did know the full story of the coastal lights, and now that the keepers are gone, there's no one to work the spells."

That made Simon look up. "Spells?"

"It's quite a story—and I heard it from my uncle himself. I have to go meet my ride, but I'll tell you everything at our appointment," she promised.

"I want to hear all about it." Simon handed her his card. "Just call and tell Pete to book you."

She headed toward the front doors as Sally Anne Roberts, the community events manager of the garden, walked over to Simon's table.

"You had a great crowd." Full of excitement, as usual, Sally Anne's enthusiasm for the garden and her job always brightened Simon's day. He was a regular during the fall, especially in the run-up to Halloween, when his books about ghosts were especially popular.

"Thank you for having me and promoting the event."

Sally Anne grinned. "We're a good team. Did you sell some books?"

"More than usual. Maybe with fall coming, people are stocking up." Simon started to put his remaining copies into a plastic box. "By the way, do you know the woman who just left?"

"Mrs. Brighton? She's a regular, especially around the holidays. Why?"

"She wants me to do a séance for her uncle, the lighthouse keeper. I wondered if you knew the history involved." Simon kept the comments about spells to himself, but he intended talk to some of his sources.

"Her uncle was the last lighthouse keeper for the Georgetown Light before it was automated back in the 1980s," Sally Anne replied. "Before that, all the lighthouses had live-in keepers."

Simon made a mental note to research the lighthouses of the Carolina coast. Something in Mrs. Brighton's comment pinged a half-remembered detail about protective magic.

"Are you ready for Halloween?" Simon asked as he and Sally Anne walked out to the main lobby.

"As ready as I ever am! It's great that we have so many community programs—readings, craft days, children's costume events, and a fall festival—but it's an all-hands-on-deck sort of thing, and when it's done, we swing right into the holidays. The good thing is that people come to the garden and see what we have to offer."

Simon thanked her again for setting up the reading and promised to come back again during the Christmas season. Once he got into the car, he couldn't stop thinking about Mrs. Brighton's words.

"Hey, Pete," he said when he called the store. "Has anyone called to request a séance?"

"Just got a call. You must be psychic or something," Pete joked.

"Or something. Mrs. Brighton?"

"Right again. What's up?"

"She was just at my signing, and she said she wanted a séance. Did she tell you anything about who we're going to try to talk with?"

"Just that her uncle was a lighthouse keeper, and she wanted to reach him. Why? Something going on?"

"I'm not sure," Simon admitted. "When is she coming in?"

"This afternoon at two. Anything you need me to do to get ready?" Pete asked.

"No, thanks. I'm going to see what I can find out before then. I think this might be bigger than just missing a departed relative."

"Gotcha. It's been quiet here, so if there are things you need to do, I'll hold down the fort," Pete told him.

"Thanks—I think I'm going to take you up on that. See you in the morning." Simon ended the call and drummed his fingers on the steering wheel as he drove, trying to decide what to do next.

He called Father Anne Burgett and smiled when she picked up on the second ring. "Simon! Great to hear from you. Please tell me this is social and that the world isn't in impending peril."

He laughed. "Well, I'm always glad to talk with you, but I can't promise about the peril. I need to pick your brain or get your St. Expeditus folks to do some research."

"Spill. We're always up for a good challenge." Father Anne was an Episcopalian priest and a member of the St. Expeditus Society, an order of clerics who researched and fought supernatural threats. Even though she was based in Charleston, she had helped on other cases.

Simon told her about the motorcycle club deaths first, including the disappearance of the most recent victim.

"You sure know how to have fun," Father Anne replied. "That's...wow. Definitely not something I've heard before, but there's a thread to it that does seem familiar. I can have someone do some digging in the archives. What next?"

"Is there such a thing as lighthouse magic? Especially on the Carolina coast?" Simon filled her in on Mrs. Brighton's mysterious comments and the upcoming séance.

"Interesting question. I'm not sure, but it wouldn't surprise me. The lighthouse keepers fit the traditional role of guardian, which pops up in folklore as a very important, almost sacred, trust. In the olden days, the keeper position was hereditary, and there were families who approached it like a priesthood."

"I can see that. After all, they were saving lives," Simon responded.

"Saving lives, sending light into the darkness, protecting the coast from threats—human and not. And before modern weather equipment, the first to warn about incoming storms," Father Anne pointed out. "Lighthouse keepers also lived a somewhat monastic life. Some had families, but many were single people who didn't mind being isolated. They had to be sturdy to maintain the lighthouse and its grounds and fearless because they weathered fierce storms. I've never researched it, but I wouldn't be surprised if some, if not all, of them had protective magic."

"That's what I'd like to know. If so, did they work alone, or did they cooperate to provide stronger protection?" Simon hesitated. "And were they just concerned with keeping people safe from bad weather or other kinds of threats?"

"Ooh, I like where this is going." Excitement was clear in Father Anne's voice. "I can't wait to see what we find out. Do you think the lighthouse issue ties together with the motorcycle deaths?"

Her question caught Simon by surprise until he remembered that he had mentioned the biker situation in an email looking for insights. "I hadn't until you brought it up. I guess it depends on what kind of creature is behind the curse on the club and whether the keepers protected against that sort of thing."

"I'll get the researchers working right away," Father Anne promised. "I'll let you know when I've got something."

Simon thanked her and promised to get together the next time he was in Charleston. Their conversation raised more questions in his mind than he expected and opened up possibilities he hadn't considered.

His next call went to Miss Eppie, a powerful root worker who had helped him on many occasions and knew the area's lore.

"Sebastian, it's been a while. What have you gotten up to now?" Miss Eppie was about the same age as Simon's mother and one of the few people who used his real first name.

"It's…complicated. We should probably get Gabriella in on this too. How soon can we get together at the Botanica?"

Miss Eppie laughed. "I just happen to be there right now with Gabriella having a cup of tea. You come this way, and we'll fix one for you."

"Thank you." Simon felt better just knowing his friends had his back. "I'll be there shortly."

Botanica Hernandez, Gabriella's shop, took up an unpretentious older building on one of Myrtle Beach's side streets. A bell rang as Simon opened the door, and he felt a frisson of magic when he stepped inside.

The air smelled of candles, plants, fragrant woods, and herbal products. Bunches of dried herbs hung from hooks on the walls.

In the back of the shop, a beaded curtain separated the break room.

"Simon! So good to see you. Please, come in. We have coffee as well as tea." Gabriella stretched out the last word like it was a bribe. She knew Simon liked that hers was often extra strong, brewed the Latin American way.

"Great to see you! Sorry I haven't been by since the honeymoon. You know what the last weeks of the season are like," Simon said. "And I will never turn down your tea."

"Hello, Sebastian!" Miss Eppie called from behind the curtain.

Gabriella turned to her assistant, whom Simon guessed was a grandchild or niece. "Call if you need me," she told the young woman. "But if anyone asks, I'm in a meeting."

Both women hugged Simon, and Gabriella fixed his tea, something she insisted on because, according to her, no one else could make it just right. Gabriella brought out a plate of cookies and set it in the middle of the table. Simon accepted the cup gratefully and closed his eyes with the first few sips, enjoying the smell and taste.

They waited patiently until he sighed and opened his eyes. "We've got a situation. There's a powerful entity that might be immortal doing death curses, and I suspect that there's magic involved with the lighthouses along the coast."

Neither Gabriella nor Eppie looked surprised. "Tell us what you know," Gabriella urged.

Simon laid out what he had told Vic about the motorcycle club deaths and recounted the latest disappearance. He caught them up on what he had learned from Father Anne and the comment from the woman at his book signing.

"I don't know what we're dealing with," he concluded. "And I'm worried because people are dying."

"You did right reaching out to Father Anne," Miss Eppie said. Even though the priest was based in Charleston, she had worked with them on other cases. "Her people at the Society have good resources."

The St. Expeditus Society had its own compound with a church, dormitories for the monks, and a large library of esoteric and occult books. Many of the books were centuries old and exceptionally rare. Some were protected by spells and wardings.

"I thought you might know more, so here I am," Simon concluded.

"It's interesting that the person who contacted you today wants to reach someone at the Georgetown Light," Miss Eppie said. "That lighthouse sits on an island that doesn't allow visitors. It's always been a place of power. During the Civil War, quite a few escaped slaves found sanctuary there and wove their own protections."

"The native peoples also thought that the locations of several key lighthouses were places of natural power." Gabriella's power as a bruja and potioner drew on the traditions of the Latin American countries of her family heritage. "They believed there was a sentient primal essence to the land, like a genius loci but more of a creature than a nexus."

"What kind of creature?" Simon asked. He reached for a cookie and took a sip of tea.

"The stories vary." Eppie picked up the tale. "The people brought here from Africa were more attuned to the spirits of nature than the Europeans were. Their beliefs recognized those spirits instead of denying or banishing them. They were willing to work with natural energies. So they adjusted their rituals and turned to them for help escaping oppression."

"It's said that a seven-pointed star can be traced between the seven most supernaturally-charged lighthouses in North Carolina. In South Carolina, the lighthouses are in more of a straight line, and creating a magical link between them was used to protect the coast from storms, reduce the creature's power, and bind it as much as possible," Gabriella resumed the tale.

"And that knowledge was passed down from one lighthouse keeper to the next?" Simon asked, fiddling with the tablecloth as he listened.

"Yes. It was a solemn calling, and the keepers had magical power as well as knowledge about the sea," Gabriella said.

"So when the lights were automated, the keepers left their posts," Simon supplied. "Who maintained the wardings?"

Gabriella shrugged. "I've heard that the keepers tried to sustain the protections, but there were no new guardians chosen to replace them, and many have died without choosing an heir."

"It would be nice to know what form this entity takes. I did some research, and there's a pretty short list of creatures who do deals and have magic that can make people disappear," Simon said. "I also need to figure out if it has other tricks we haven't discovered yet."

"That is an unusual combination," Eppie agreed. "Which tells me it's very old magic. I'll see what the ancestral stories say."

Gabriella nodded. "I'll look into it as well and let you know."

"Thank you. We need to figure out how to defeat or bind the entity and restore the protections around the lighthouses," Simon added. "We might not be able to eliminate the creature, but it sounds like there were ways to keep it from running amok."

They talked for a while about the upcoming Halloween events, the change in the weather, and the grandchildren that Eppie and Gabriella adored. Simon told them about his and Vic's honeymoon in England and was amused at their questions about adjusting to married life.

"You know that being gay-married is just like regular-married only gay, right?" he laughed. "People are people. I lay my bets that there's more similar than different in the whole adjustment thing."

Gabriella chuckled. "You're probably right about that. And neither of you are teenagers. Back in the day, we got married young and had to grow up while we figured out how to be a couple at the same time. With babies. It was quite the juggling act."

"Lord, I don't miss those days," Miss Eppie said. "I was tired all the time."

The alarm on Simon's phone went off. "That's my cue to go meet the lady from the garden event. Thank you for letting me come over and for the tea. Any research or ideas you come up with, please toss them my way."

Gabriella made a shooing motion with her hand. "Let you come over? You know you're welcome here any time, and your young man too. The tea's just part of being sociable."

"Don't worry—you've got us interested now," Miss Eppie added with a laugh. "We'll dig into this like bloodhounds. I've already got some people in mind to talk to."

Simon thanked them again and headed for his car.

He thought about his conversation at the botanica. Simon appreciated the different perspectives that Gabriella and Miss Eppie brought to their discussions that opened investigations up to a much broader range of possibilities.

People tend to think that the US was just a blank slate before the Europeans got here, but of course it wasn't. There were people with their own cultures and religions who knew the land. Monsters lived here, and there were ancient places of power. We didn't listen to the people, so we found out the hard way about the monsters and places.

Sometimes, those old creatures break loose and go wandering. Is that what happened with the bikers' deal? And was it a side effect of the coastal lighthouse magic or a direct result?

Simon couldn't shake the feeling of being watched, even though he didn't spot any likely culprits. He grabbed a burger at a drive-through and ate it after he parked in his usual spot near his shop. Simon scanned the lot before stepping out of his warded car, being extra careful.

A truck veered toward him, seemingly out of nowhere. Simon had no room to flee. He heard the screech of brakes, the smell of burnt rubber, and the overwhelming pain of impact as bones cracked and flesh tore...

As quickly as the vision hit, it vanished. Simon nearly lost his footing and caught himself against the hood, breathing hard. He couldn't fight the urge to pat himself down, finding no injuries, no wreck, no truck.

He looked around but didn't see a likely culprit. Even so, Simon's sixth sense told him this was a warning and that he had attracted the entity's attention as a potential foe.

It took a couple of minutes for Simon to catch his breath and for his heart to stop pounding. Simon thought about calling Vic to warn him but realized he didn't know what to caution him about. Simon had been the target of the vision, and it wasn't hard to guess that the entity wanted him to stay out of its business. He debated calling

Vic and decided to hold off until later since it had been a vision and not a real attack.

He took the long way back to the store and picked up fresh coffee for him and Pete.

"Oh, thank Cthulhu." Pete cradled the coffee cup in both hands. "I was afraid of nodding off. It's been extremely quiet today."

"Never say that," Simon replied, only partly joking. "The universe will decide to make sure you're not bored."

"Everything go okay?" Pete asked as Simon leaned on the counter and flipped through the email on his phone. "Your reading at the garden ended a while ago."

"I grabbed a quick lunch and visited with Gabriella and Miss Eppie," Simon confided. "The motorcycle bargain was weird enough, but now I'm wondering where the lighthouse fits in."

"If it does," Pete warned. "It seems like a stretch."

Simon filled him in on his discussion at the botanica. "Actually, a connection isn't as weird as I thought. Especially if it's a case of old magic trying to contain an ancient creature." For now, until he could figure out the entity's role, Simon held off talking about the vision.

"Okay, rookie question here, but are there two entities?" Pete asked. "The being that does deals and makes people go poof, or the lighthouse magic that draws on some big-deal old energy? Are they both sentient? How old are they?"

Pete took a sip of his coffee. "If they're magic, what kind of magic? If they were here before the Europeans came, were they also here before people came over the land bridge from Asia? And if so, would we even recognize what kind of magic they use?"

Simon grinned. "Nothing rookie about any of those questions. They're damn good—and that last one worries me. What if the magic for the guardians and the power they draw from pre-dates any culture we know? We like to think that everything important waited until there were people around to notice, but the world was off doing its thing for a long time before humans showed up."

"If there are dinosaurs involved, I want in," Pete said.

"I don't think we're dealing with dino magic," Simon replied, pretty sure Pete was just joking.

"You never know. Maybe they could do spells, and someone goofed, and that's what set off all the volcanos," Pete embellished with a grin.

"Let's hope that there aren't any volcanos involved—or dinosaurs," Simon replied with a shiver.

They looked up when the bell over the door rang, and Mrs. Brighton entered. "I know I'm early, but I wasn't sure about parking."

"Come right in," Simon said. "Would you like a bottle of water?"

"That would be lovely. Thank you."

Simon took his cup to the break room and returned with bottles for all three of them. "This is Pete, who keeps everything running here while I go galivanting around at libraries and gardens," Simon told her, and she shook Pete's hand.

"Pete, this is Mrs. Brighton, who called about the séance."

"Please to meet you, ma'am. I'll make sure you don't get disturbed."

Simon ushered Mrs. Brighton to the back table and waited while she put down her purse and got seated. He guessed she was in her seventies, with silver hair in a flattering cut. A navy blue jogging suit gave her a sporty look.

"Thank you for working me in so quickly. I know it was an imposition to ask."

"It's not always possible, but when we can, we try to accommodate." He looked more closely at Mrs. Brighton than he had been able to in the aftermath of the event at the sculpture garden. Simon wondered if she was sleeping well. She seemed to have a lot on her mind.

"I was very close to my uncle when I was a girl. He never married. Went to the Navy for a while, and when he came back, he took the job with the lighthouse. Most people weren't allowed to visit the island, but of course we were. He and my father were brothers and had a strong bond even though my father got married and had a family. Uncle Frank said that his nieces and nephews were just like having his own kids."

"Did you ever see anything supernatural or even just a little weird when you were visiting?" The idea of live-in lighthouse keepers seemed so different from modern times.

Mrs. Brighton got a far-away look in her eyes. "There were things he took for granted that, in hindsight, probably weren't normal. Even on hot days, parts of the lighthouse were as cold as a refrigerator. Now and then I heard a child laughing when we were alone and there wasn't any radio or TV.

"One night, there was a bad storm. All of a sudden, Uncle Frank wanted us to have a sing-along. He and my dad looked spooked. I thought I heard screaming, but they told me it was the wind." She gave a sad smile. "I don't think that was where the noise was coming from."

"You believe the lighthouse and island are haunted?"

Mrs. Brighton nodded. "Yes. And both Uncle Frank and my father knew it. My dad let me visit, but he made me wear a crucifix necklace—and we weren't Catholic. I would find loose salt in my pockets and little bags of iron nails tucked into my suitcase. I don't think Uncle Frank would have knowingly put me in danger, and my father trusted him to protect me, but I think he took precautions, just the same."

"Did you ever get the sense that there was anything else… weird…about the lighthouse? Did being at the lighthouse feel different from other places?"

She considered for a moment and then nodded. "One summer I got my parents to visit different lighthouses. They didn't all feel like the Georgetown Light. The closest thing I can compare it to is what it's like to walk into an old church, one of the big cathedrals that has been around for a long time. There's an energy you can't put into words."

Simon understood what she meant—the sense of being on consecrated, protected ground. Whether those wardings were religious or magical, people with sensitivity to the supernatural could often pick up a sense of power.

"I can't promise that I'll be able to contact your uncle or that if I do, he'll answer. Sometimes ghosts aren't social. We'll call out to him and see what happens."

"I understand. In all the years since he passed away, I never tried to seek out his ghost," she said. "I wanted him to be at rest. But I'm getting a strange feeling, like there's a storm coming, only not regular weather. Something…other. The kind of thing that wouldn't have happened if Uncle Frank and the other lighthouses were keeping up the protections."

"How did you find out about the wardings?" Simon couldn't help being curious since it didn't seem like something that would have come up casually, especially when she was younger.

"One night there was a storm brewing and a full moon. I came downstairs to get a glass of milk, and I saw Uncle Frank standing outside the lighthouse in the rain. He was talking, but there was no one else around. Then I saw him cut his palm and let the blood drip onto the wet concrete, and he shouted something in a language I didn't understand."

"That would have been frightening to a child," Simon sympathized.

"He came in soaking wet with a towel wrapped around his hand and realized I had seen him. I asked what he was doing—I wasn't afraid. I loved and trusted him. He said he was praying for safety. And I guess, in a way, he was," she said. "Only invoking magic, not talking to God."

"When did you figure that out?" Simon asked.

"Much later. He wanted to stay at the lighthouse until he died, but his health didn't let him carry out the duties anymore, and the state wanted to automate. He told me he worried about what would happen without keepers—only the way he said that the word definitely had a capital K like it was a guardian, not just a job," she recalled.

"Did he tell you why he was concerned?"

"He was very sick when we talked about it, and on medication. I'm not sure he would have said what he did if he were his usual self. He kept mentioning the seven-point star lighthouses in North

Carolina and the chain in this state, and how without the wardings, the energy wouldn't contain the danger," Mrs. Brighton answered.

"Did he ever tell you what that danger was?"

"No. I didn't press because he was fading, and I wasn't completely sure how his mind was, especially with the medicine. But I wish I had. I've always wondered if he took a shine to me because I had some of his talent. And lately, I feel like there's another storm on the horizon, not the normal kind. I don't know what to do."

Simon gave his best reassuring smile. "Well, let's see if Uncle Frank will answer and take it from there."

"Are you ready?" Simon asked. Mrs. Brighton nodded, and Simon tightened his grip slightly.

"Frank Brighton, can you hear us? Your niece wants to speak with you." Simon spoke quietly but with authority. They waited. This was the difficult part: waiting to see if the spirit would respond. Simon could ask, but it was up to the ghost whether to respond.

"Uncle Frank? It's me, Millie. Please come. I have an important question about the lighthouse."

Simon felt a presence stir in the distance, reaching toward them.

"I think he's listening, but he's still far away," Simon told her. "Ask again."

"Uncle Frank—I need your help. It's about the protections."

The ghost drew closer, and its energy shifted, growing stronger as if waking from slumber.

"Ask your question," Simon urged. "See if he responds."

She nodded. "Thank you, Uncle Frank. I've missed you. I need to ask you what to do because the protections from the lighthouses are fading. People are disappearing. Is there a way to restore the wardings even though no one lives at the lighthouses anymore?"

They waited. Simon strained to listen for any response from the ether.

"Find my journal for my first year in the lighthouse," Frank's ghost said, and Simon relayed the message since only he could hear the spirit. *"There are notes…invocations…instructions. I was getting older. Didn't want to forget. Then I worried that there was no one to pass along the knowledge. I left it to you because I hoped you would understand."*

Mrs. Brighton smiled despite tearing up at Simon's recount of the ghost's response. "Yes, I have it. I haven't read it…just never seemed the right time."

"You will need help. One lighthouse isn't enough. Best to get a descendant, otherwise need witches."

"What is the energy the lighthouses keep at bay?"

"We called it the Wellspring because it was old and deep. It was part of the land. That's why it could keep the creature contained."

"If we can raise the wardings again, will it be able to keep the creature at bay?" she asked,

"As I understand it, yes," the ghost replied. Simon could tell the spirit was tiring.

"What is the creature? Where did it come from?"

The ghost paused long enough that Simon wasn't sure it would answer.

"It calls itself Trogre."

Simon's heart sank. "Trogre? I've heard that word before."

"What does it mean?" Mrs. Brighton asked.

Simon met her gaze. "Troll."

4

VIC

"Troll? Are you fucking kidding me? Like the ugly toys with the green hair?" Vic responded.

Simon waited him out. "Not really. Trolls are one of the most ancient creatures in stories from across the world and most cultures. They are magical, they can shapeshift or make themselves invisible, and they can make people disappear."

Vic paced behind his desk while Ross watched with amusement. "Seriously?"

Simon filled him in on what he had learned that day and the séance. "That's what the last keeper of the Georgetown Light believed the guardians and the Wellspring kept at bay. I'm guessing the Wellspring—the energy around the lighthouses—is a type of genius loci, but I need to confirm that. I'm headed to do some more research. The ghost thinks we can restore the wardings. We'd just need our own team to keep them refreshed."

"You make that sound easy."

Simon paused, and Vic knew his husband was waiting out his mood. "The original wardings were maintained by lighthouse keepers who weren't witches. They weren't necessarily descendants, although a few lighthouses did pass from father to son to grandson. That means that the magic can probably be done by anyone who understands the necessary powers involved."

Vic sighed. "Okay. That's not the weirdest thing we've ever done."

"Thank you—I think."

"And we've discovered something else," Vic went on. "We looked at disappearances around Myrtle Beach since the lighthouses stopped being manned. There are a lot."

"Not surprising, given that it's a beach and there are a plenty of people who come through here who might be looking to start over. We both did."

"We didn't disappear—we relocated. Kept the same names, changed jobs, and people knew where we went," Vic noted. "I get what you're saying—some people might have plans to erase their footprint and become someone else. But even accounting for that, over the years, there's a higher-than-average rate for a city this size. So we're looking into it. I hate to say it, but if we rule out everything else, it's probably something woo-woo."

"Mrs. Brighton is looking for her uncle's journal. She inherited it but hadn't felt comfortable reading it. Now that we know he recorded his ritual there, it's a start," Simon replied. "There's also a big collection of everything to do with the lighthouses at St. Cyprian College. That'll be the next step once we know what Frank wrote."

"There are a lot of lighthouses just in the Carolinas."

"Apparently only seven in North Carolina count to anchor the magic, and all the ones in South Carolina. Georgetown is first on the list. I'll let you know what I find out. And I'm planning to be home for dinner."

"See you then. Be careful. Love you," Vic said.

"Right back atcha. Love you too."

Vic turned to see Ross looking at him. "Trolls?"

"They're badass in the old stories. Let's not mention it to anyone until Simon does his research-fu and we have more to go on."

"Where do we go from here?" Ross reached for his coffee cup, found it empty, and grimaced.

"We work this like any other case."

"Except it's got a troll."

"We've dealt with worse people."

"True."

Vic started to pace again. "The motorcycle club made a deal to stop a gang war. Maybe the other disappearances weren't as random as they seem, even if they aren't tied to a decades-long bargain."

"What do you have in mind?" Ross got up to fill his coffee cup and realized the pot was empty. He started another one as they talked.

"I think we find out whatever we can about the people who were never found. Some of them still probably have family and friends who are alive. Find out why they ran or what they were escaping. If they were escaping."

"We don't want to give the families false hope," Ross pointed out. "We aren't likely to find their loved ones, even if we figure out who took them."

Vic nodded. "Yeah, I know. But if there's a pattern to why those particular people were taken, we might be able to help Simon decipher the magic. And if we can do that, we're working the case from the other end. He'll gather what's needed to bring back the protections, and we can figure out who's vulnerable."

Ross sighed. "Okay. Let's get to it. But you're buying me dinner soon for making me do dialing for dollars." That was what Ross called the process of calling people from a list to gather information, one of the things he hated most about the job.

"I'll even spring for beer because I'm that awesome of a partner," Vic joked.

Ross printed out a list and they split the pages, then got comfortable before they started calling.

Vic looked down the list, only a portion of the full roster of the disappearances from the past forty years. Ross had done his best to sort by age, but there were other variables as well, especially last known address and prior police record.

It didn't escape Vic how many of the missing people had no

known next of kin or contact listed. Serial killers often preyed upon people no one would miss, and he wondered whether monsters were savvy enough to do the same.

After an hour and dozens of calls each, they compared notes.

"Each of the family members I talked to said that their person was down on his luck—and it's all men, by the way," Ross said. "Lost a job, got divorced, bad breakup, going bankrupt, poor health diagnosis. They didn't know for sure what made them come to Myrtle Beach, but they figured it was to get a fresh start and cut ties."

"So maybe the motorcycle guy was an outlier, making a deal to benefit someone else. Maybe the people most likely to be taken think that anywhere is better than here," Vic mused.

"Not always true, but I can see why people might think so."

Vic tapped his fingers on the desk as he thought. "Simon said the creature could shapeshift. So maybe it switches to human form to size up its victims. Hangs out in bars. Maybe it can literally smell desperation."

"Plenty of human serial killers and grifters do that—I'd think that something with magic would be even better at it," Ross suggested.

"We don't know what happens next," Vic said. "Does it follow them and suck out their soul? Do they need to make a deal or ask for a favor? It might just get the jump on them like a regular predator, but in a lot of the old tales I've heard Simon tell, there's usually something transactional, even if the victim doesn't realize it at the time."

"Did any of the people you talked to say that someone had looked for the missing person?" Ross asked.

Vic shook his head. "No. They might have been related to the victims, but there wasn't any real attachment. Pretty sad, actually." He and his large family weren't always in agreement, but Vic always knew he was loved.

"And more common than we like to admit," Ross said. "I keep thinking that the connecting thread is that each of the people who went missing had gotten themselves into a jam they didn't see a way to fix on their own. If you're desperate enough to think about changing your name and running away, you've run out of good alternatives, and you're ranking the bad ones."

"Ditching everything and going missing is one step removed from just checking out completely," Vic remarked. "Maybe the creature can spot the ones who got separated from their herd, so to speak. Less risk."

"That's giving the creature a lot of credit, don't you think?" Ross leaned back and stretched.

Vic thought for a moment. "Is it? Wild animals are smart enough to take on the prey that stray from the group, lag behind, or are too weak to put up a fight. The creature we're talking about might not even have to worry about health—like with Carter Edwards—because it's not consuming the body—just the soul."

"Eww," Ross protested. "TMI."

"Hey, I grew up watching all those nature shows with my brothers. Wildlife is brutal, man."

"Has Simon tried to contact the ghosts of the people who vanished? If the creature sucked out their soul, would they still be around as a spirit, or would they just be, I don't know—erased?" Ross asked.

"Yes, they were ghosts, but fading according to Simon." Vic looked at the list again. "Okay, we can't do magic, but we do data— which is almost the same," he said, and Ross snorted. "Hear me out. Let's plot the last known locations. It might help us figure out where the creature is doing its hunting."

"If it can look like anything, how do we catch it?" Ross asked.

"I'm going to leave that up to Simon," Vic replied. "He was headed to some college library to do research. But I figure this is a legit part of our job since it's people who are victims of a crime in our territory. And if Simon's right and it's connected to the light-houses becoming automated, this has been a forty-year crime spree."

Ross fed the data into a program that would map the data points while Vic scanned the printouts for anything they might have missed. No matter how good and helpful computers were, human intuition often spotted connections that defied binary logic.

Vic's phone rang. He didn't recognize the number.

"Detective D'Amato? You just called my sister about our brother, James Hinton, who went missing ten years ago."

"Can I put you on speaker?" Vic asked and got approval. He set his phone on the desk so Ross could hear. "Go ahead."

"I'm Scott Hinton, and I was with Jimmy the day he disappeared. I was trying to cheer him up. He'd had a rough go for a while. Job trouble, woman trouble, health problems. Even though he was only in his late twenties, life had beat him down. He was my older brother, and I didn't want to see him unhappy."

"What happened?"

"We went down to Ocean Boulevard to walk around and kill an evening. Get some food, have a couple of beers, people-watch and hang out," Scott said. "I could tell Jimmy was trying to get in the spirit and appreciated being together, but he was just so sad. We went to the big arcade and played games.

"We were together all evening. Then I went to the bathroom, and it was crowded so it took a bit. When I came back, Jimmy was playing pinball against a guy I'd never seen before. They were joking around, and Jimmy said, 'I bet I can beat you.' Just joshing, not even putting money on the line," Scott went on.

"He had perked up, so I didn't interfere. I went to get drinks. When I came back, they were both gone. No one saw them leave, but we never saw Jimmy again."

Vic knew that the timeframe was before security cameras were everywhere. "Did he drive? Was his car missing?"

"No," Scott said. "I drove that night. I went nuts looking for him. Got the arcade staff involved, called the police, nothing. But people said he probably just made a new friend and went to have a beer, and he'd turn up in the morning. Except Jimmy wouldn't leave me like that. We were close."

"When he didn't come back, I put up signs. Filed a missing person report. Went back to the arcade every night to see if the guy he played with was a regular. They said he often came in a couple of nights a week, but no one knew who he was." The agitation in Scott's voice made it clear that despite the years that had passed, the disappearance was clear in his mind.

"I thought maybe if he went after Jimmy, he'd go for me too if I hung around. He didn't show. Even the arcade staff said that they hadn't seen the guy since the night Jimmy went missing," Scott said. "I always hoped that Jimmy would show up out of the blue, and it would be some weird story about bad drugs and a road trip, but that didn't happen. I still miss him."

Vic could hear the pain in Scott's voice and couldn't imagine losing one of his brothers like that. Ross had stopped his work to listen and looked shaken.

"I'm sorry for your loss," Vic said. "I know it's been a long time, but do you remember anything about the stranger Jimmy played with? What he looked like?"

"That was almost forty years ago. Whatever he looked like then, he won't be the same now, if he's even still alive," Scott replied.

"It might help us match him to photographs in the system," Vic replied and crossed his fingers.

"Okay. What's stuck in my mind, even after all this time, is that he was unusually tall, like a basketball player, and pretty beefy. Plain features—not ugly, but not handsome. I think the word is rugged. Shaggy blond hair. Huge hands."

"Did you hear him talk? Did he have an accent?"

"No, sorry. I remember wondering if he was a pro wrestler because he looked very muscular."

"Anything different about his clothing?" Vic pressed, probing for some kind of lead.

"Not fashionable—just a plain T-shirt and loose-fitting jeans. I figured maybe he had trouble finding things in his size."

"Thank you," Vic told him. "I'm sorry to bring up bad memories."

"Don't be. I think about Jimmy every day. If you find out what happened to him, I want to know," Scott said. "And if you can catch the guy who took him away—make him pay."

Vic promised to keep Scott informed and ended the call. He

looked over to Ross and knew his partner could read the emotional effect of the conversation.

"If this creature is a shapeshifter, it could have come back every night looking like someone else, and no one would have been the wiser," Vic said.

"Yeah, that occurred to me too," Ross said. "Does the creature have a quota? Maybe it just eats until it's full? So, it wouldn't have necessarily returned to the arcade until it needed another meal."

"Let's keep going and see if we can get a few other stories. Then we can compare notes once Simon's done his research," Vic suggested.

They worked their way down the rest of the list. Many of the contacts had either left without a forwarding address or had died. Some were in nursing homes. Others refused to discuss the subject.

Finally, Ross got lucky. "It's been a while since anyone asked questions about Tom," Sherry Cranston said after Ross put the call on speaker. "After all this time, we finally accepted that he wasn't coming home, although he'd be welcome if he did. We still mark his birthday. It would be good to get an answer, one way or the other. Although I want to think he ran off to some tropical island and turned his life around, I don't think he'd stay out of touch if he were still alive."

"I know you've given the story before, but can you go over it for me again, please?" Ross asked. "Particularly anything you remember about people he was with."

"We went to a party at a friend's house," Sherry said. "Early Eighties—loud music, big hair. We were mostly hanging out and drinking beer. Some of the guys got up a poker game. Low stakes, just something to do.

"Tom had a run of bad luck, and I practically dragged him to the party. Told him to stop moping and that he'd feel better around people," she recounted, and Vic could hear old guilt in her voice.

"He humored me and went, but he didn't perk up until someone suggested poker. Tommy wasn't a high roller, but he liked the game. It was the most interested I'd seen him in a long time, and I knew he wasn't going to lose his shirt, so I hung out with the girls in the living room, and the guys set up a game in the dining room," Sherry went on.

"Did you know everyone at the party?" Ross asked. "Were there any new people or strangers?"

"It was our regular gang, except for one guy I hadn't seen before. I asked who he was but everyone thought he was a friend of someone else's," Sherry replied. "Big guy. Broad shoulders, thick arms, large hands. Rather plain in the face. Built like a lumberjack, although he was dressed like everyone else. Didn't say much, but he might have been the one who suggested the poker game."

Vic and Ross shared a look. *Trouble.*

"They played a few rounds, and everything seemed fine. The girls and I were just talking and listening to music, having a couple of beers. No one was making wild bets. From what I could hear, Tom seemed like he was on a winning streak. I wondered if his friends let him win to cheer him up. I heard him say double or nothing, and the new guy said, 'I accept.'"

"What happened after that?" Ross asked.

Sherry sighed. "Tom lost. He wasn't playing for much money, just for fun, but it kinda took the wind out of his sails. He went outside to have a smoke on the back steps, and the new guy went with him. We never saw either of them again."

"Nothing left behind?" Ross asked.

"Tom's pack of Lucky's, his lighter, and a half-smoked cig were on the steps. Nothing from the new guy. I know Tom didn't just take off without telling me. He never did that sort of thing, and he hadn't had more than one or two beers," Sherry said.

"Did the stranger have a car?" Vic leaned in toward the phone.

"That's the weird thing—when we couldn't find them, and everyone started talking, no one knew where he'd come from. We all thought he was friends with someone else, but we compared stories, and he wasn't. It's like he just wandered in and made himself at home and no one questioned him," Sherry recalled. "If he had a car, it wasn't parked with everyone else's, and we didn't hear him leave."

"When did you realize something was wrong?" Ross pressed.

"I had a bad feeling that night, but Tom's friends knew he'd had a rough patch and thought maybe he and the new guy just went out to a bar or to score some weed." She chuckled self-consciously. "It's been forty years—is the statute of limitations up on that?"

"We're definitely not concerned about the pot," Ross assured her. "What next?"

"When he didn't come home, I knew something was wrong. That just wasn't Tom. He would have called, and he didn't just crash with strangers. I checked in with all our friends, and when no one had heard from him or seen him, I called the police," Sherry told them.

"Since it had only been overnight, they didn't think it was a real disappearance and told me he probably just passed out watching TV and would wander back home in a while. If he'd been with someone we knew, I wouldn't have worried. But I didn't like that he'd gone off with a stranger. Anything could have happened.

"Tom didn't have much money, so I doubt it was a robbery. He was a nice boy, maybe a little too nice, which got him into some of the scrapes he was trying to get out of. Had a knack for trusting the wrong people who took advantage. I miss my brother."

Vic and Ross exchanged a glance. They might discover what happened to Tom, but returning him was unlikely.

"I know that after all this time, he's probably not still alive," Sherry said with a hitch in her voice. "But if we can't bring him home, I'd like to know what happened, and see if we can do something to get him justice."

"I understand," Ross said. "That's why we're looking into some old cold cases that might be connected. I have you on my list, and if we do find something, I'll let you know."

"Thank you," Sherry told him. "You know, Tom was the whimsical one. That's why I think life went so rough on him when things didn't work out. He loved fairy tales when he was a kid, and read all the fantasy books and saw the big movies when they came out. I think that if he could have moved into one of those make-believe worlds, he would have gone."

Uh-oh. Vic saw his reaction mirrored on Ross's face.

"If you think of anything else, no matter how small, about that night or the stranger, please give me a call." Ross made sure she had his information before hanging up.

"Do you think the troll could sense that?" Ross asked. "I can't believe we're talking about trolls."

"Same. I don't know—predators have good instincts to spot likely prey. It sounds like Tom might have begged to go without realizing the ramifications."

"Or maybe he did. The folks who've been taken were hanging on by a thread. They might have been desperate enough to think that anywhere was better than here," Ross pointed out.

"It's also possible that because the creature is a shifter, it doesn't show up on security cameras," Vic mused. "Although that can vary. Sometimes they show up with reflective eyes. Maybe it varies by the type of shifter."

It wasn't lost on Vic that not too long ago, he never would have considered anything paranormal a remote possibility. *Simon changed everything—and I'm so glad he did.*

"Is there a pattern to the disappearances the creature is responsible for?" Ross wondered aloud. "There are non-supernatural reasons people go missing. But I'm wondering if the troll eats his fill, so to speak, and then sits it out for a while before binging again. If we could find a pattern, maybe Simon and his friends could—I don't know—do something witchy to keep it from happening."

"I think that's what he's working on right now from the other end of the hypothesis," Vic said. "Without the lighthouse keepers, we'll need to create a surrogate set of guardians who maintain the wardings. I'm wondering if there's a Supernatural Coast Guard like there seems to be a paranormal version of everything else."

"They probably don't have a website," Ross replied with a straight face.

"Ya think?" Vic snarked. "But Simon's cousin, Cassidy, should be able to find out, and if she can't, her hacker buddy, Teag, probably can."

In the years since Vic had gotten clued in about the supernatural, he had come to appreciate a network of people with abilities who used their talents to protect the coast while staying well under the radar of regular law enforcement, the media, and most of the government. While it was great to know they existed if needed, figuring out how to contact secret organizations did pose a challenge.

Vic and Ross spent the rest of their shift calling on cold cases. They turned up several with similar stories—large stranger makes a bet, person vanishes without a trace. Vic plotted them on calendars, looking for any patterns.

"I shouldn't be surprised, but there are clusters around the solstices and the equinoxes," Vic noted. "The fall solstice disappearances extend to Halloween, which would be a time no one would pay attention to strangers or someone who looked a bit off."

"Before the lighthouses were automated, with the records that survived, there's no clear pattern, "Ross noted. "The creature could still slip one through now and again, but the wardings definitely cut down on the frequency. The people who disappeared back then, when the guardians were active, seem to be plain ol' regular missing persons. Some of whom did eventually show up—dead or alive—later on."

"We can't track every person on the coast who's gone missing in the last half century," Vic said. "But let's look for the same seasonal pattern of disappearances around the lighthouses in that time period. That should be reasonably easy to run a database search on."

Once again, Ross ran the searches while Vic made more coffee and brought over a reasonably fresh, half-empty box of cookies.

"Even with narrowing the search, that's still forty years of data," Ross said. "I'm going to run one now and set the rest to run overnight. They'll process faster because the network won't have as much traffic, and they should be ready in the morning."

"This makes me wonder—is there a Supernatural National Park Service that keeps tourists away from Bigfoot? A lot of those parks are on land that the native people have considered sacred or at least paranormally active for a very long time," Vic added.

"Not our jurisdiction," Ross said without looking up from his keyboard. "Don't make this huge job any bigger!"

Vic laughed. "Okay. Do you want me to take a lighthouse? Would that help?"

"How about as I get one data set gathered, you go through it looking for clusters, and I'll move to the next lighthouse? That way we won't trip over each other."

"No guarantees about that, bro, but fine with me."

They worked past quitting time. Captain Hargrove came by and frowned. "Shouldn't you boys be headed home?"

"Just closing up for the night. Following up on a lead," Vic told him. "We think there may be a pattern to solve some old cold case disappearances, and we're trying to close in on the perp." He decided to hold off on the woo-woo angle for now. Hargrove supported Simon's involvement, but Vic didn't want to strain his boss's patience or put him in a tough situation to defend with his own managers.

"I can't authorize overtime, so you're on your own until this becomes an active case," Hargrove warned. "And I'm not responsible for angry spouses when you let dinner get cold. Otherwise, knock yourselves out."

An hour later, Vic's phone pinged, and he checked a new message from Simon. "He's wrapping up at the library, and he'll be home in half an hour. Want to find a stopping place for tonight and pick this up tomorrow?"

"Sure." Ross blinked rapidly several times. "My eyes are going blurry. But I put a couple of data sets in to process, so that should be a quick read on whether we're on to something."

They walked out to their cars. "Thanks for believing all this crazy stuff," Vic said.

Ross grinned. "Hey, it makes life a whole lot more interesting—especially when it also explains stuff we couldn't figure out. I'm down with it."

Vic waved as Ross drove away and walked toward his motorcycle. The hair prickled on the back of his neck, and he had a strong sense of being watched even though he didn't see anyone around.

His right hand went to the gun on his hip, while his left touched the silver charms Simon insisted he wear. When nothing moved and no one stepped out of the shadows, Vic headed toward his bike, parked near a shoulder-high brick wall. Vic climbed on the Hyabusa just as a loud cracking noise drowned out its engine.

A deep crevice appeared in the wall and spread along its length. The bricks tumbled, denting hoods and breaking windshields of the cars parked close.

Vic zoomed out of the way just as a brick sailed past his head, landing with a thud on a car right behind him.

That brick didn't fall. It was thrown.

Car alarms blared, and people poured from the headquarters building, swearing over their damaged cars and pointing at the strange damage to the wall.

Vic stuck around to answer questions and scan for clues, but he couldn't provide any information beyond what he had seen. He didn't know much about building walls, but nothing about what had happened seemed normal.

Does the troll know I'm Simon's partner? Would it have a way of knowing we're looking into the disappearances? Was that a warning—or an attack— meant for me because we're asking questions? Or was it a way to get to Simon by hurting me?

Vic drove more cautiously than usual, alert for danger on his way home, but he only encountered normal traffic. He beat Simon to their blue bungalow, so he got the mail and started making a quick dinner. Vic thought about the fallen wall, still not sure what to make of it; he'd check the police report in the morning. Until he had a better idea of whether it was shoddy workmanship versus anything supernatural, he decided not to mention it to Simon.

Being comfortable enough to cook a good meal was one of the many things Vic loved about being married versus dating. He still wanted Simon to think well of him and tried to do nice things just because, but Vic no longer felt the need to make every dinner or evening out a memorable occasion.

When they were both tired, take-out or spaghetti was perfectly acceptable. And if they were exhausted after a day at work, crashing on the couch with a favorite show was better than a fussy date.

Tonight though, they had plans to check out the local Boo and Brew event on the boardwalk, even if they didn't stay late. The seasonal programs were fun, and Simon felt an obligation as a local business owner to be supportive and visible.

We're not complacent. We're real. I never understood the difference before, but now I do. And I absolutely love what we have together.

5

SIMON

"Thanks for granting me access on such short notice." Simon followed the special collections librarian at St. Cyprian College down a long, narrow corridor in the stacks of the research room.

"Thank *you* for brightening up my rather dull shift," Mrs. Ames, the research librarian, said with a conspiratorial grin. "It's not every day people come looking for information on trolls."

Simon fought the urge to cringe and looked around to see if anyone was listening. He still couldn't quite believe the turn this case had taken. "I appreciate you taking my request seriously."

"Our saint is the patron of occult and mystical practice," Mrs. Ames replied. "It takes a lot to surprise us." She leaned toward him. "My hair didn't used to be gray until I started working here," she added with an impish grin.

Mrs. Ames looked to be in her late fifties, with dark skin and short-cut silver hair. "I like a challenge, and this isn't a topic anyone's ever asked me to look into."

To Simon's relief, she didn't ask the reason for his interest. He was still trying to wrap his mind around the possibilities himself.

"You know, I always think of trolls as European entities." She led him deeper into the stacks. "I forget they're organic to the world, not to any particular geography. They show up under one name or another in pretty much every folklore."

As they passed the carefully shelved books, Simon swore he could sense glimmers of power from some of the tomes. When he concentrated, it sounded like voices whispered on the edge of his hearing. Along the wall, special runed boxes and carved wooden cases fitted with elaborate locks made him wonder what dangerous books or materials they held.

Mrs. Ames brought him to a section across from a large wooden reading desk with an antique brass library lamp.

"Here you go—these three shelves should be our collection on trolls. Most of the books are in English. None of them require special handling—arcane or otherwise. Did you bring acid-free gloves?"

Simon nodded. "Yes, ma'am. Plus plenty of pens and paper." Graduate school had trained him in the etiquette of rare book rooms.

He already felt at home in the archive. The air smelled of wood, aged leather, and the very particular tang of old paper.

"Very good. Come get me if you need anything. I'll reshelve the books—just leave them on the desk."

"Do you have any favorites on this topic? Somewhere you'd suggest I start?" Simon had learned long ago that librarians were the Indiana Joneses of hidden knowledge, and a few good questions could save hours of frustration.

"Unless you're looking for general background, I'd focus on the accounts based in Canada and the United States. Of course, the Kaplan Turner books are classics, but they take a rather broad brush and so while they're good for background, I think you're looking for something a bit more focused."

Simon nodded. "Ideally, I'd like to find older works that are less mythologized, that treat trolls like rare beasts instead of fanciful creatures. To be honest, I'm more interested in something like a game warden's handbook than colorful folktales."

Mrs. Ames adjusted her glasses and gave him a look that made Simon wonder if she had some psychic talent. "You're looking for something tactical, not just scholarly."

He tried not to squirm, hoping she wasn't about to lecture him on taking things too seriously. "I'm looking into a pattern of disappearances over a period of years that doesn't match normal circumstances. And when something doesn't fit into the natural order, it requires moving farther afield."

To his relief, she didn't laugh. "That helps. Disclaimer—many of these books are very old. While some of them have taken the tone of cultural anthropology, the authors might just have been gifted storytellers. I'd start with these."

She went down the shelves with a practiced eye, selecting books with faded covers until she had half a dozen on the reading desk.

"The Ormondson brothers are what I've always described as what you'd get if you crossed Hans Christian Anderson with Jane Goodall," she told him. "Part fabulist and part neutral observer. Whenever I read the Ormondson books, I have the feeling I'm reading fact slightly disguised as fiction."

"The investigation has hit several dead ends pursuing normal leads. We're hoping that taking a different tack might open up other possibilities." Simon didn't want to fuel speculation, but he needed the librarian's help, and she seemed predisposed to be more accepting than he had dared hope.

"Hamlet was right about there being more things than we've dreamt of." Mrs. Ames's smile told him she enjoyed being on the hunt. "If there's anything else you can tell me to help you narrow the selections, I promise to keep it in confidence."

She dropped her voice. "I've always believed librarians function under the seal of the confessional."

Simon glanced around, confirming they were alone. "There's a pattern of recurring disappearances that may be linked to an old bargain with a troll."

"You mean like that odd motorcycle accident everyone's talking about? The one where the rider just up and vanished?" she asked.

"Among others. You can imagine that the media would make hash out of anyone looking into trolls to explain it."

She nodded. "Your secret is safe with me. This is a college dedicated to the esoteric and arcane. That wouldn't be the oddest thing anyone has ever researched here."

Simon didn't think he wanted to know what counted as strange if trolls in Myrtle Beach didn't. "Thank you."

"The two-volume work by Sanders might be good, too," she added. "It gets into some of the details that might seem less exciting on the mythic side but important for practical reasons. For example, trolls can't make people disappear on a regular basis. It takes too much out of them. So there's a recharge period between disappearances that provides a chance to attack."

"Interesting," Simon replied, reaching for the books she mentioned. "We were trying to figure out how to confront one without getting poofed."

"Good to consider," she said, although he sensed that his wording amused her. "If I recall correctly—and please verify this before you go into battle—they still have some formidable abilities short of killing someone. Like distorting time and sending nightmares."

Simon shivered, unconsciously clutching the books a little tighter. "That's something I need to know more about."

"Make yourself comfortable at the desk. There's a button that will buzz my station if you need help," Mrs. Ames pointed out. "As usual, no eating, drinking, or marking in books. Cell phone photography is permitted for personal use, but please do not post your photos publicly without permission."

Simon thanked her and made himself comfortable at the old wooden library desk. The stacks were quiet, but he didn't sense any dangerous energies. Simon felt more at peace in the library than anywhere else except the beach.

The Sanders books proved remarkably readable for scholarly tomes, and well-organized. Simon felt his heart skip a beat as he read more about troll magic.

The legends vary about the recharge period—the stories say it differs by the species of troll. But the odds are good that we're safe from being disappeared for at least five days after the last person was poofed. Give or take. Might not want to push the margin on that.

So the clock is ticking.

He read further and caught his breath.

Trolls can make walls and buildings collapse. Good thing the house and shop are warded. I wish I could ward the police station too.

He had done his best, with Vic's help, to add what magical protection he could, but being a public building ruled out some of the spells.

Nightmares and phantom pain don't sound like fun. I bet the vision I got was the troll trying to make me back off. We're fairly safe inside the house and store, and the car is warded, but everywhere else, we're only as protected as the charms and amulets we wear can provide.

Does the troll know I'm after it? Can it sense my abilities? I don't want to endanger people by going to public events like the Boo & Brew if the troll is out to get me.

Then again, it can't wreak too much havoc, or it drains its power and makes people more wary.

Still, good to find out that it can't zap an unlimited number of people into oblivion. I want to stop the troll, but I have no intention of getting killed over it or letting that happen to Vic or our friends.

He looked up, feeling watched, and saw an elderly nun at a distance. She wore the traditional all-black head covering and loose robe, and the intensity of her stare made him wonder if she disapproved of his visit.

When he blinked, the nun was gone.

Before he had a chance to think further about his visitor, Simon's phone vibrated, and he saw a text from Vic.

Vic: *Any luck?*

Simon: *Maybe. Just sitting down with the books now. Give me a couple of hours. How's your day?*

Vic: *Quiet so far. Don't want to jinx it.*

Simon: *Still on for dinner and then the Boo-and-Brew?*

Vic: *Counting on it. Be careful. Love you.*

Simon: *The risk of getting hurt in a library is low, but never zero. Love you.*

Handling any supernatural case around Halloween always made Simon think about the thin line between myth and reality.

Witches, psychics, vampires, were-creatures, ghosts, and other paranormal creatures were real, as was magic of all sorts. But just like television and movies presented a glamorized portrayal of doctors, detectives, and other real-life high-risk professions, the fictionalized version of supernatural gifts left out the less sexy parts like years of study, hours of training, and endless repetition to get a ritual exactly right.

Or spending most of the day in the stacks at a library, Simon thought as he set out his pen and notebook and started on the first tome.

Simon never had reason before to read up on trolls in particular, so all he knew was from fairy tales from his graduate study and movies. While there were some nods to the idea of gnarled creatures that lived under bridges and lusted for treasure, many of the older stories spoke of shapeshifters that could blend in with regular people and had magic that could alter people's perceptions to see things that weren't really there.

In some accounts, trolls lived peacefully near regular humans, offering their tremendous strength to help with chores. They married and raised families and were exceptionally gifted with needlecraft.

I wonder if there's something with Teag's magic that might help, Simon wondered, thinking of his cousin Cassidy's friend who was an accomplished weaver-witch.

As for trolls spiriting people away, some accounts said there was little hope to reclaim the missing people. Others suggested prayers, ringing bells, or using steel and fire to reclaim those taken.

There's not much here about bringing people back after they've been taken. The few cases that are in the stories didn't work well.

Time passed quickly, and before Simon knew it, the alarm on his phone buzzed, warning him to gather his things before the library closed. He had filled most of a notebook and taken dozens of pictures in lieu of copying large sections of texts.

"Did you find what you were looking for?" Mrs. Ames came up behind him so quietly that Simon flinched. "Sorry—didn't mean to startle you."

"That's okay—I just really got into the material," Simon told her. "You've got a fantastic collection here."

"We're very proud of it," she replied. "And seeing as it's under the auspices of the church, it's protected."

"I made a note of which books I was using in case I need to come back. This has been tremendously helpful."

"I'm glad." Mrs. Ames frowned. "I hope that you're not thinking about trying to get someone back who has been taken. The scholars who drew from the oldest sources believed that trolls took people who didn't want to be found. Almost like a supernatural relocation program. All the noise about trolls eating people made sure most people left them alone—except for those who needed their help."

Simon felt certain that Mrs. Ames had some arcane talent of her own, whether that was highly tuned intuition, some psychic abilities, or a touch of magic.

"I picked that up from the text. It puts an interesting spin on the tales," Simon agreed.

"The old versions of the stories are much more…nuanced," Mrs. Ames said. "The trolls in them aren't just brutish ogres. They have families and societies. Most of our modern impressions come from a book written in the mid-1800s. That leaves a lot of room for interpretation."

It wouldn't be the first time the Victorians fucked up a perfectly good folktale, Simon thought. Thanks to the printing press and a wider distribution of books, the more modern versions soon overtook the oral traditions.

The local troll isn't that beneficent. We already know he takes a life for losing a bet, replenishing his energy. Figures we couldn't get one of the helpful trolls.

"Are there nuns here? I saw one in the stacks but she didn't speak. I had the impression she might not have welcomed my intrusion." Simon was still curious about his visitor.

Mrs. Ames's eyes widened. "Nuns? Not for a very long time. They were instrumental in the founding of the university, but over the years, there are fewer of the sisters and brothers, and those who remain are largely retired."

"Any visiting nuns doing research?" Simon knew what he had seen. Mrs. Ames didn't seem completely surprised.

"Some of the early monks and nuns were utterly committed to the university. It was their life's work. As you know, that kind of bond can make it difficult to let go and move on."

"So the university is haunted?" Simon pressed.

"Oh, yes. We welcome the sisterhood and brotherhood emeritus, as we call them," Mrs. Ames said. "They are a cloud of witnesses and our protectors. We acknowledge and thank them on all formal occasions, and both students and faculty invoke their protection and support. The library has a few who we assume never wanted to leave their books behind."

Simon described the ghostly nun he had seen, although her habit didn't leave much for identifying details. "She was short and very slightly built. Quite elderly, with a thin face and high cheekbones."

"Ah, you've met Sister Petroula." Mrs. Ames nodded. "She helped to assemble the library and was so devoted to it that she often slept on a pallet in the office after late nights cataloging books. Rumor has it she had some magical abilities and wove protections around the books and the library to keep them safe. She probably sensed your talents and came to see why you were in *her* space."

"I hope I passed muster," Simon replied. "And I like the idea of the library and university having a group of spirits protecting them. Please pass along my thanks to Sister Petroula for allowing me access."

"She has a habit of making the water pipes bang if she disapproves, so we'd have heard by now. I think you passed." Mrs. Ames laughed.

"I found a lot to think about," Simon added. "I took pictures of the books so I know what to come back for. They've been very help-ful. Thank you."

"Any time. We have several friends in common. I've wondered when you would finally find your way here," she said with a myste-rious wink.

Simon checked his watch and found himself looking forward to the Boo and Brew event, despite how much his normal work centered on ghosts and the supernatural. Simon didn't have any difficulty separating the fictional ghosts and horror stories from the real paranormal. Sometimes people who didn't believe in the super-natural meddled with things they didn't understand and got hurt, but for most people Halloween was a time for beer, candy, costumes, and parties.

"Dinner's ready," Vic told him when he opened the door. "Spaghetti. Figured we'd eat early and then go check out the Boo and Brew."

"Sounds wonderful. I'm starved—and I'd rather not completely fill up on bar food," Simon replied, hanging up his jacket before he went to the table.

"And here I thought I'd have to start without you," Vic teased.

"You must have come home early," Simon replied, checking his watch.

"Oh, baby. I always come right on time." Vic dropped his voice.

"I'll take you up on that later," Simon said.

"Count on it," Vic flirted back.

They ate quickly and headed for the festival. Simon was just as happy to have time to process what he had learned at the library before trying to add it to their theories about the troll, and he resolved to enjoy the evening despite the case.

The Boo and Brew was a boardwalk party with music, chances to win prizes, and plenty of people in costume. All the drinks had horror-movie-inspired names, and most were green, purple, or orange for the occasion.

"What are you drinking?" Simon noted the concoction in Vic's glass.

"It's a Virtual Vampire. No clue what that means, but it tastes like a vodka martini with a little juice in it."

Since they were walking home, Simon ordered a Zombie Brain Transplant, a mix of gin and something pink.

All the appetizers had been creatively renamed, and it took a moment to figure out the menu. They were regulars, so Simon trusted the bar's food to be good, but he still wanted to know what was going to end up on his plate.

"Anything interesting happen today?" he asked Vic when they finally had their drinks, and there was a break in the music.

Vic shrugged. "Cap didn't have anything else pressing for us to work on, so Ross and I are still looking into the disappearances. The pattern holds steady—people who were unhappy and wanted to escape."

"Lots of people fit that description, but they move to a new town, get a tattoo, or buy a sportscar," Simon pointed out. "They don't completely and permanently vanish without a trace."

Despite what Hollywood suggested, wiping away a person's digital and real-life footprint wasn't easy. Even espionage professionals didn't always succeed. Dropping out of sight might have been simple before cameras, DNA, and social media, but the modern world meant a person's movement could be tracked and recorded without them knowing, removing the evidence from their ability to erase.

"I don't think the trolls are eating people," Simon remarked as he took a mozzarella stick—called a zombie finger in the event menu—and dipped it in sauce. "I think they gain from an energy exchange when a person crosses the threshold between here and there, but they aren't literally consuming humans." He told Vic about what he had found out regarding other ways trolls could cause harm short of killing someone.

"Knocking down walls?" Vic echoed.

"Yeah, why?"

Vic sighed and told Simon about the incident when he left the precinct. "I was fifty-fifty on whether it was a shoddy retaining wall or something supernatural."

"Pretty sure after what I read today that it was a warning—or an attack." Simon shivered at Vic's close call.

"Splitting hairs, don't you think?" Vic dipped a chip into hot queso.

"Split hairs can make all the difference in magic." Simon shrugged. "I had a strange thing happen to me too."

Vic listened as Simon recounted his vision.

"God, Simon. Please don't take any chances," Vic said when Simon finished.

"At least mine was just a premonition," Simon replied. "A wall actually fell on you."

"It missed."

"Close enough," Simon countered.

"Back to the troll," Vic said. "Why is it so different from the stories we've heard?"

"It's possible that what came down to us through the Victorian folklorists glommed several legendary creatures together and added their own details to make a better story. Tales about a solitary nature creature aren't as thrilling," Simon answered.

"But they make people disappear," Vic protested.

"If they only choose people who want to vanish, there's a level of intelligence beyond a creature that simply kills for food," Simon answered. "If we can reinstate the lighthouse protections, we should be able to stop the disappearances."

"Except there aren't lighthouse keepers anymore. So how does that work?" Vic countered.

"One thing at a time. I'm still figuring it out." He didn't mention how much it bothered him that the troll had clearly connected him and Vic and that the link endangered Vic. They set the case aside for the rest of the evening, listening to the music, remarking on costumes, and enjoying the beach party vibe of the event. Even though summer was over and winter was fast approaching, Myrtle Beach never lost its vacation vibe despite cooler temperatures. Simon understood why some people preferred the shore when days were more moderate and crowds thinner.

Each night of the Boo and Brew featured a different local band.

Simon nodded along with the music as he and Vic finished their food and nursed their cocktails. Myrtle Beach had strict open container laws, so the party couldn't spill out onto the boardwalk. That didn't stop people from dancing to the music outside the large, open windows.

The air smelled of smoke from the tiki torches, beer, and more faintly, weed.

Simon realized Vic was watching him with a soft smile. "What?"

"It's nice to see you look relaxed. Even if it doesn't last long."

"Just enjoying the music—and the company." He let his hand brush Vic's, enough to make the connection.

The party continued until midnight, but Simon and Vic left not long after ten. They both had to get up for work in the morning, and the second band wasn't a favorite.

Despite the late hour, lots of people still walked the boardwalk even though the beaches themselves were closed.

Simon spotted someone he recognized and turned to call out to them, but they had already passed out of range.

"Something important?" Vic asked.

Simon shook his head. "No. I saw one of my Skeleton Crew who I haven't seen in a long time. I'll give him a call tomorrow and check in."

Over the years Simon had been in Myrtle Beach, he had attracted a small following of younger people with fledgling psychic gifts who could use a mentor. Although he steered them to others suited to teaching their focus, Simon kept in touch and encouraged them to explore their abilities and learn to manage what they could do. He had jokingly referred to the group as his Skeleton Crew, and the name stuck.

Once they left the boardwalk, the music faded, overshadowed by the hum of traffic. Despite the well-lit route back to the bungalow, Simon and Vic remained alert. Crime wasn't rampant in Myrtle Beach, but it was wise to be wary, and the troll threw a dangerous wild card into the mix.

Simon couldn't shake the feeling of being watched. Vic didn't seem to sense anything amiss, and Simon trusted his husband's cop instincts. Still, Simon's intuition also took in paranormal elements, which Vic didn't always note. He remained wary even if he couldn't pinpoint a threat.

If the troll is a shapeshifter, he could look like anyone. Does he know I'm looking into his history? Would he care? Myrtle Beach has had plenty of psychics and witches that have come and gone. The troll is still here.

Will he attack if he suspects we want to renew the binding? Or is the deal sufficient enough that he gets what he needs, regardless?

"Hey, I know that look." Vic bumped Simon's shoulder. "We're off duty. Quit thinking about work."

"You gonna give me other things to think about?"

"When we get home. Don't want to get arrested for public indecency," Vic joked.

Despite Simon's concerns, nothing interfered with their walk home. Simon made sure to do extra wardings on the doors and windows once they were inside. Vic watched him, saying nothing until he was done.

"Something up?"

Simon shrugged. "Couldn't shake the feeling that we were being watched. Might just be my nerves."

Vic took Simon into his arms. "Well, if something is watching, how about we give them a real show?" He kissed Simon, starting slow and then adding tongue, letting a hand slide down Simon's chest.

Simon returned the kiss, tugging at the hem of Vic's T-shirt and pulling it over his shoulders. Simon's shirt soon joined it on the floor, and he walked Vic backward toward the bedroom.

Many nights, they started their lovemaking in the living room on the couch watching television. Tonight, for reasons Simon couldn't put into words, he didn't want slow and lingering; he needed hot and fast, proof of life.

"Don't know what's gotten into you, but I like it."

They tumbled into bed, a tangle of limbs. Simon thumbed open the button on his jeans, got them halfway unzipped, and pushed them and his briefs off as Vic hurriedly shed his clothing.

"Want you on top," Simon murmured, pulling Vic into his arms, kissing him open-mouthed and hungry.

"Any way you want it." Vic ran his hands over Simon's body. They explored with fingers and lips and mouths for a while, licking and stroking until touch became an exquisite caress.

"Want you in me," Simon breathed. "Need to feel you move."

"That can be arranged," Vic chuckled in a low rumble.

By now, they knew each other's favorite spots, and Simon shivered as Vic kissed his jaw and moved down the column of his neck, then let his tongue tease at Simon's nipples as his hand slipped between Simon's legs to fondle his cock and balls.

"Oh, yeah." Simon brought his hands up to stroke Vic's back and grip his ass.

Sometimes they could stretch out lovemaking for hours on lazy weekends or vacation days. Tonight, Simon wanted connection and release, needing to feel Vic's fingers dig into his biceps and relish the stretch and burn of taking his cock even after they came.

Vic seemed to sense Simon's mood and took control, which Simon willingly relinquished. One of the things he loved about their partnership was how equally they balanced roles, able to switch back and forth, leading and following in everything, not just in bed.

Now, he let pleasure banish worries and drive repetitive thoughts from his mind. Vic knew what Simon liked and how to turn his crank. Simon reached for Vic's cock, and Vic gently batted his hand away.

"Let me drive for now," Vic murmured. "I've got you." Vic took his time prepping Simon, opening him carefully and slicking the way. Preparation was part of the pleasure.

Simon knew how lucky he was to have a partner who knew him so well and accurately read his mood. He gave himself over to being loved and letting arousal drive all other thoughts from his mind.

"That's it," Vic coaxed. "Just feel."

Simon wrapped his legs around Vic's waist, and Vic slid inside, pausing for a few seconds fully seated and then starting a slow, regular rhythm. Simon let his head fall back, completely open to Vic, focusing on the growing intensity of sensation.

Reaching climax didn't take long, and Simon arched as his orgasm overtook him. Vic's hand stroked him through the orgasm, sending sticky ribbons of come to paint his chest. Seconds later, Vic's hips jerked, and he followed him over the edge.

They lay tangled together for a moment, just breathing, enjoying the afterglow.

"That was…perfect." Simon kissed Vic on the temple.

"Yeah." Vic sounded just as blissed out as Simon felt.

Reluctantly, Vic eased out and rolled to the side, handing Simon a fistful of tissues and using another wad to help clean up.

"Better?" Vic asked as he tossed the bundles into the trash.

"Uh-huh." Simon floated in a post-orgasm haze and wasn't in a hurry to lose the moment.

"Good." Vic licked a stripe up the middle of Simon's chest with the flat of his tongue and then kissed him on the lips. "If that didn't distract you, we can try again. I have a few more tricks."

"Mmm. Definitely did distract me, but I won't turn down your tricks." Simon knew he sounded spent.

Vic got up and went to the bathroom, then returned with a warm, wet washcloth and wiped Simon down and then himself, and lobbed the cloth toward the doorway. "Shower in the morning?" His voice was a low rumble that made Simon want to go again, despite his sated body's desire for sleep.

"Definitely. After round two," Simon pulled Vic in for another kiss.

"Promises like that could make me into a morning person."

"I can make that happen." Simon did his best not to lose the afterglow, keeping his thoughts in the here and now and pushing aside anything to do with lighthouses and trolls.

In the morning, after a spirited round of wake-up sex, Simon fixed scrambled eggs and bacon while Vic showered.

"Anything going on at the shop today?" Vic poured them both cups of coffee.

"Things always get busy in the lead-up to Halloween." Simon plated the eggs and brought them to the table. He settled in across from Vic and smiled when Vic's first bite yielded a pleased moan.

"I'm still looking for the details of the protections that lapsed when the lighthouses were automated." Simon paused to dig into his breakfast. "Once Mrs. Brighton finds her uncle's journal, I was wondering if you'd take a road trip with me to check the South Carolina locations."

"Certainly." Vic made short work of his eggs, nibbling at the last piece of bacon. He refilled their cups as Simon worked through the food on his plate. "What are you hoping to find?"

"From the journal, clues about the old protections and rituals and what it would take to activate them again without full-time lighthouse keepers. From the road trip? I'm not sure except that sometimes you get a lot of information from the feel of a place, even when you think you've read everything about it."

"Worst case, we don't find anything paranormal and we have a nice day driving up and down the coast. Works for me," Vic assured him.

Simon's schedule of readings and séances kept him busy most of the day. In between customers, he mapped out the route to the lighthouses and searched for nearby sites that might dampen or amplify supernatural power. They might not be able to check out everything in one trip, but Simon wanted to try to take as many factors into consideration as he could.

For fun, he also noted possible restaurant stops and nearby roadside attractions to break up the drive.

Most of his appointments that day related positive news to clients, either from his psychic read of their situations or from the ghosts contacted in the séance. Simon preferred days like that to times when the interactions did not go as smoothly, or the connections shared disappointing information.

Still, a full calendar of doing psychic readings or using his abilities to contact spirits left Simon tired by the end of the afternoon, despite Pete's diligence in bringing him coffee with cream and sugar throughout the day to keep up his energy.

More than once Simon got up and glanced out the shop window, looking up and down the street.

"Expecting someone?" Pete asked.

Simon shrugged, a little out of sorts because he couldn't articulate what prompted his actions. "Not really. I just can't shake the feeling of being watched."

"You think someone is staked out to keep an eye on us?"

"That's just it—I haven't seen anyone suspicious loitering around. So my imagination might just be getting to me," Simon admitted. "But it doesn't change the way it feels."

"Go with your gut," Pete replied. "I'll refresh the wardings, just in case."

Simon's last client had just left when Mrs. Brighton arrived. "Sorry to catch you late in the day, but I thought you'd want to see what I've found so far."

Simon ushered her to the table as Pete flipped the sign on the door and started closing the register.

"My uncle considered being a lighthouse keeper a holy obligation, like the priesthood," Mrs. Brighton said. "I would follow him around whenever we visited and ask questions. He never seemed to mind."

"I know the decision to automate the lighthouses was out of your uncle's control. But do you think your father would have followed in his footsteps if the lighthouse had not been automated?" Simon asked.

"Oh, no," she replied. "My father made it clear early on that he had other plans. He went to college and only came back for holidays. It's not something most folks are cut out for. More of a calling."

Simon could understand. With computers, cell phones, satellite television, and the internet, living at a lighthouse wouldn't be as isolated as before modern times. But the lack of day-to-day, face-to-face connection wasn't for everyone.

"He kept a journal and made notes every day—we found boxes of them, one for each year. This is the one his ghost wanted me to find, the one he mentioned in our séance as his first year at the lighthouse. He noted the weather and the ships that came by, as well as the wildlife. I think he loved being able to see the birds and dolphins. He left the journals to me.

"But one was set aside—for the first year he was at the lighthouse," she went on. "I think it was because it had information about how to maintain the wardings and what rituals he needed to do to keep them strong."

She pulled the old leather-bound book from her purse and passed it across the table to Simon. "Maybe you'll make more of it than I could. To me, the pretty verses sound like a prayer, but I guess I don't understand how these things work."

Simon's fingers traced the leather, getting a frisson of old memories and faint power.

"It's not so far off thinking of them as prayers, but not meant for a particular listener," Simon told her. "More like speaking to the universe itself, using the words to harness the speaker's will and intentions, an act of creation by voicing something into being."

"That's very poetic."

Simon shrugged. "It's a deeply-rooted reaction at the core of every belief system, so it touches something in how we're wired. I can't explain it, but I'm not going to discount something that old and powerful."

"He makes comments in his first journal about how important it is to keep the wardings strong, do the ritual on a regular schedule, and not skip over anything in the incantation," Mrs. Brighton said.

"And he mentions something I didn't expect. The South Carolina lighthouses are in a pretty straight line down the coast. But the North Carolina ones are a little more spread out. According to his notes, seven of those are more supernaturally powerful than the others, and it's possible to draw a seven-pointed star in a circle using them as the key points."

"A pentagram in a circle is an old protection sigil," Simon mused, acknowledging the validation of the story he had heard. "Probably not something they bring up on the lighthouse tours."

She laughed. "No, I'm sure they don't."

"Thank you for sharing this with me," Simon told her. "I'll take good care of it."

Mrs. Brighton laid her hand over Simon's. "Do with it whatever you need to do to bring back the protections. I know that's what my uncle would want."

"Would you mind if I digitally scanned it? That way it's preserved for the future."

She gave a vague wave. "Fine with me. That sounds like a good idea. For as important as the wardings seemed to my uncle, it's a bit scandalous that they've just gone by the wayside."

"Thank you." Simon gripped her hand gently. "I think this is going to be very useful."

"I'm glad to help. I hope everything goes well." She waved goodbye to Pete and left the shop. Simon watched from the window until she was out of sight.

"I'm going to put the journal in my bag and shut down my computer," Simon told Pete, who had nearly finished closing. He had barely gotten to his office when he heard someone rapping at the front window.

"It's Ricky," Pete said when Simon came up front. "What do you want me to do?"

Simon glanced at the clock and figured one more conversation wouldn't make him too late for dinner. "Let him in. And if you don't mind, stick around, please. We won't be long."

"You've got it." Pete headed for the door, unlocked it long enough for the newcomer to enter, and locked it again afterward.

"Sorry to come so late," Ricky said. "But I heard something I think you'll want to know."

Ricky was one of the Skeleton Crew, but Simon hadn't heard from him in a few months. His untrained ability as a medium had sent him spiraling until Simon helped him get the training he needed to manage his gift and control his abilities.

"What's up?"

Ricky rubbed his hands on the front of his jeans, a nervous gesture that went with his twitchy way of looking around even though the shop was empty except for Simon and Pete. "I've been working at the shelter for the last six months. It's part of qualifying for my certification, but I really like it there. I feel like I'm helping people."

After Ricky had gained more control of his mediumship, he had been able to go back to school. He was working on a counseling certificate and hoped to be able to steer others with paranormal abilities to resources that would help them learn about their gifts instead of writing them off as imagination.

"Beach towns get a lot of drifters," Ricky said. "People down on their luck, looking for a fresh start, or who just give up and plan to fade away by the ocean."

Simon could relate, having come to Myrtle Beach after his personal and professional life exploded. He had been fortunate to have the resources to rebuild. Not everyone was as lucky.

"So we have our regulars and our newbies," Ricky went on. "Some of them keep their distance, but the ones that stick around, we get to know at least a little. Unless they get picked up by the cops for vagrancy or stop at a soup kitchen, we're likely to be one of their only points of contact."

Simon nodded. He quietly kept track of the younger psychics he mentored, knowing that without a support system, their gifts could be overwhelming.

"We don't track our clients. But we notice when they aren't around for a while. I got talking to James, one of the other volunteers, and we realized that a couple of regulars haven't been in for several weeks or longer. That's unusual for them."

"Maybe they moved on? Found a better situation?"

"Maybe," Ricky said. "And I hope that's true—but that's not what my gut says."

Simon took intuition seriously. "What do you think is going on?"

"The guys who haven't come around are hard cases. No family, no real social connections. Most of them have serious health conditions that aren't getting treated—lung cancer, that sort of thing. They're marking time until they check out," Ricky went on. "We try to steer them into residences and other programs, but it's up to them whether they stay. Some of them like being loners."

Simon felt a prickle on the back of his neck as he guessed where Ricky's tale might be going. "What's changed?"

"For one thing, the ghosts that hang around the neighborhood seem edgy. I know it's silly to talk about dead people being scared—"

"Not at all. Spirits can be preyed upon by some supernatural creatures," Simon mused.

"That's—not comforting. Anyhow, I noticed that I hadn't seen some of our regulars for a while. It's not like we can check up on them. But we're a free meal and a hot shower and a place to watch TV for a couple of hours, so clients have a reason to come back," Ricky said.

"I made a list—for what it's worth. I don't even know last names for most of them, and the names I do have might be fake. I think they've gone missing, and no one else has noticed."

Simon picked up troubling vibes the longer Ricky talked.

"These are folks at rock bottom. They didn't have bus fare, and I don't think anyone would pick them up hitchhiking. I asked the ghosts, thinking that maybe some of the clients just died somewhere and got taken away as John Does," Ricky said. "None of their ghosts answered, but the spirits that hang around got real freaky."

"Freaky—how?"

"Like they were scared and didn't want to talk about it. What scares ghosts?"

Really bad things. Simon could think of a number of entities that could scare spirits, usually with the threat of consuming them. The troll would definitely qualify.

"I think you're onto something, but that's a difficult group to prove someone has gone missing," Simon replied.

"I know, which is why I didn't go to the cops. Here's my list." Ricky slid a folded piece of paper across the table to Simon. "I'm sorry I can't suggest how to find them."

Simon took the paper and put it in his pocket. "I can check the John Does at the morgue and the vagrancy arrests. Also the involuntary commitments. My husband is a cop—he should be able to access the information. It's difficult without full names, but we might be able to account for some of them. If they just moved on, there's no way to tell."

Ricky nodded. "I know. And I hope that's what happened. But when I ask my intuition, I get that Magic 8 Ball answer, outlook not so good."

Privately, Simon agreed. *If the troll wanted to break the truce without getting caught, that's the group to target. And if he just makes them disappear, there's nobody to find, no proof. I'm getting the same feeling as that Magic 8 Ball.*

The disappearances happened over time, so maybe the creature sneaks in a snack when he builds his power back up. The trick is going to be catching him at a low point.

Having a store along the beach and boardwalk meant Simon had gotten a crash course in homelessness. People who fell on hard times found their way to the beach, looking for a second chance or hoping to tune out. During busy seasons, the demand outstripped the town's resources and services.

That could provide a banquet to a creature like a troll that chose targets no one would miss and left no evidence behind.

"Thanks for letting me know," Simon told him. "We'll take it from here. Please don't go investigating on your own."

Ricky crossed his heart. "No need to say that twice. But I'll let you know if I hear anything else."

Simon let him out the door, locking up afterward. He and Pete gathered their things and headed out.

"You think the troll is grabbing some extra meals?" Pete asked.

Simon winced. "Yeah. Predators are usually good at knowing how to pick off the ones that won't be missed. There's no way to issue a warning without sounding like a crackpot. We'll have to figure out a way to stop the troll."

He walked Pete to his car. "Remember, I'm going up the coast with Vic tomorrow, so I won't be in. Call if you need me."

"Sure thing. Be careful, okay? I have to admit, this whole troll thing freaks me out."

You and me, both, Simon thought. "I'll do the best I can. Thanks for holding down the fort."

He still couldn't shake the feeling of being watched, although there was no one in sight. Once Pete was gone, Simon drove home, lost in thought about what to do about the missing people and how in the hell they were going to stop a troll.

Simon stayed alert for the short drive. The car was warded, so he knew no one had placed a hex bag or laid a spell on it. While he was inside the vehicle, Simon benefitted from the additional protections.

Is the troll watching me, or have I freaked myself out? How did he figure out that I might be a problem—and what does he think I can do to him? If there's a way that I really can pose a threat, I'd like to know what it is so I can make the troll stop killing people.

He glimpsed a tall, raw-boned, broad-shouldered man standing on the sidewalk near an intersection on Ocean Boulevard. Seconds later, just as Simon's car approached the crossing, someone yelled a warning, and the traffic signal poles swayed, toppling to the ground along with wires and a steel pole as bystanders screamed and horns honked.

Simon practically stood on the brake to get stopped without hitting anything, and he braced for impact in case the drivers behind him weren't as quick. Tires squealed, but the cars managed to stop without a collision.

Two cars were pinned beneath the toppled poles, which made deep dents in the roof and trunk. He couldn't see whether the drivers were injured. Pedestrians congregated on the sidewalk, and a few gawkers approached the damaged cars, checking in with the occupants.

Simon's heart pounded, and for a moment he couldn't breathe. On the other side of the wreckage, he spotted the tall man who fit the description of the troll that Vic told him about, pieced together from witnesses. The man stared directly at him, smirking. Simon reached for the door handle, but the troll stepped back into the shadows and vanished before Simon could get out of his car.

He settled back into his seat with a frustrated grunt, trapped in the snarled traffic until the police and ambulances arrived. Simon slowed his breathing and collected his wits as sirens blared.

With the protective charms, the troll can't come at me, Vic, or Pete and Ross directly. The shop and house are warded, as well as the car and Vic's motorcycle. So the troll has to threaten in a different way—by showing he can hurt bystanders because he knows that might slow us down.

Magical extortion—"nice beach town you've got here, sure would be a shame if anything happened to it."

Simon knew they couldn't afford to let the troll carry on unchallenged, despite the danger. *This means we have to find a way to shut him down fast before he hurts other people or figures out a weakness in our protections. The game has changed—and it's a race to the finish.*

6

VIC

"**I**'d like Halloween much better without the Devil's Night angle." Ross settled into his chair after getting a fresh cup of coffee.

"We don't get the brunt of it like the uniforms do," Vic reminded him.

"Unless they get overwhelmed and we get dragooned."

"Ooh, fancy word! Are you watching one of those historical series, or is that a word-a-day calendar thing?"

Ross flipped him the bird. "As you can see, I am equally fluent in sign language."

As homicide detectives, Vic and Ross got pulled into crowd control when the rest of the precinct was overwhelmed. Since it usually only happened a few times a year during large events, Vic didn't mind too much, especially since it came with overtime.

On the other hand, dealing with rowdy tourists involved everything Vic didn't miss about being a beat cop.

"I think Cap sends us in to keep us grateful for detective jobs," Ross said.

"You might be right, although we're not exactly rays of sunshine."

"We work *homicide*, Vic. No one really expects that."

"How come the rowdy tourists get a misspent youth? We didn't," Vic mused. Growing up in a family of cops meant either his parents or his older brothers kept close track of him. Getting out of line wasn't an option.

"I grew up in a tiny town. Everyone knew my parents. If I ever dared to do anything, word would have gotten home before I did, and there'd have been a reckoning," Ross replied.

Thanks to good crowd management, the Halloween revelers didn't get too out of hand. Drunk and disorderly arrests were plentiful, along with some minor vandalism, loitering, and littering citations. Pickpockets and petty theft went along with people in big crowds being tipsy. A very visible police presence helped to discourage altercations, and bar bouncers shut down arguments before they became brawls.

All of which was well and good, but being the sober person at the party was never a fun role.

"Is Simon planning to do his thing again this year?" Ross asked with a wave of his hand to indicate that Vic would understand what he meant.

"You mean the usual wardings, protections, raising of protective spirits, and witchy, Voudon and Hoodoo spells to keep the dark energies at bay? Yes. I hate to think what October would be like without them." Vic's initial skepticism had given way to a deep and sincere appreciation of the role Myrtle Beach's supernatural protectors played in quietly helping to keep the peace and avert harm.

"You and me both," Ross replied.

Vic's computer pinged, and he downloaded the file that arrived.

"What's that?"

"A hunch. I know we went through all the missing person reports, and it looks like the troll is abiding by his truce. But my cop radar doesn't believe it. If we haven't found a paper trail, maybe the troll is smart enough to pick people who won't be noticed."

"I think you're probably right, but I'm not sure how we prove it," Ross said.

"I'm working on that part. I figured I'd start with the usual caseworkers, shelter staff, night shift folks. Ask who hasn't been around in a while, and figure out who just moved on and who disappeared."

"That's a thin line with the folks at rock bottom," Ross said. "So many of them are totally disconnected—no family, no friends, no attachments. We usually only know something went wrong when we find a body. But without that—"

"Yeah, I know. Makes the perfect crime. The troll is ancient, so he knows where to look for easy food and not get caught. Then again, maybe he prefers healthier stock."

"What are you hoping to find?" Russ settled in with a fresh tablet and pen.

"Honestly? I'm not sure. Maybe it's a dead end. But I've got a hunch the troll is too hungry to just stick to his bargain, especially if he can cheat. That way he gets one assured meal without angry people hunting him, and there's nothing stopping him from snatching extras that won't be missed."

"Even if we put a list together of suspected missing persons, we can't prove the troll did it."

"No," Vic admitted. "But if he's taking people, then we aren't breaking the truce to go after him. The same way we'd go after a serial killer targeting the same group."

"Does this have something to do with rules of magic?"

"I guess it does. According to Simon, the real thing is different from most of what's on TV. There are rules of engagement and etiquette that are taken very seriously. Breaking them can cause serious penalties."

"We're talking about a troll. Super old and very powerful. Why would he care?" Ross sounded skeptical but interested.

"He made a pact to keep from being hunted. If he breaks the bargain, all bets are off."

"Could Simon and his friends kill the troll?" Ross looked intrigued.

"I hope we don't have to find out. But if he's right about the lighthouse keepers being guardians and having something to do with protecting the Grand Strand, then maybe there's more than one way to limit the damage the troll can do," Vic said.

"Here's how I understand it—although Simon might snicker at my translation," Vic continued. "When the lighthouse keepers started their protections, it put limitations on the troll, even if it didn't kill him. That kept him from overfeeding. From something Simon found out, he can't make people vanish over and over without taking a break in between to recharge, which works in our favor. Except we don't know for sure how long he takes to power back up or when the timer started over again. Many decades later, the motorcycle club offered him guaranteed meals without repercussions, and whether in good faith or bad, the troll took the deal—not long after the lighthouses became automated."

"Maybe he always planned to cheat. Or he waited to make sure that the keepers—guardians—were really gone before he started to break the deal. If he's really ancient, perhaps in the past he had a different deal to clean up the vagrants, and as long as he took the people no one missed, the hunters didn't intervene."

"Harsh."

"But possible," Vic argued, and Ross shrugged in acknowledgment.

A couple of hours working their contacts yielded a list of several dozen possible disappearances going back a few years.

"None of them were on the missing persons list we started with," Vic noted when he and Ross finished their calls. "Their habits weren't regular enough for anyone to be sure they hadn't just gone off on their own accord—wherever off might be."

Police work involved seeing the good, the bad, and the ugly of human nature—and the places where community and government systems failed. Non-profits did the best they could with the resources they had, but there was always the need for more. Too often, bad people—or creatures—exploited those gaps, knowing it would be easy to avoid detection.

"I don't know whether to be furious or depressed," Ross confessed. "I wish the community could do better. But I don't know how to fix the problems."

"Yeah. Same. Which means we just tackle the little corner that we can affect and take it as a win." Making peace with a broken system was a survival skill cops learned early. Not being able to ignore the consequences drove plenty of them to drink.

"How do you think this is going to play out?" Ross asked. "If we can't kill the troll, and he won't keep the bargain, does he just keep taking people?"

"From everything Simon's found, during the years that the lighthouse keepers were guardians and worked their wardings, it reined in the troll. That's what we're hoping to find out more about tomorrow, visiting the sites," Vic said.

The coffee maker beeped, and Ross got up to refill their cups. He snagged them both a couple of cookies from a tray before coming back.

"But there aren't lighthouse keepers anymore," Ross pointed out.

"I don't think that running the lighthouse is the main point or that automating the light matters," Vic replied. "Simon's still figuring it out, so I could be wrong, but I think it's having someone at those places with strong energy keeping the protections fresh that counts. The places of power are ancient, but it's pretty common, I guess, for people to pick up on that subliminally and build a church, a shrine, or some sort of protection on the site."

"Which came first—the lighthouse or the protections?"

Vic shrugged. "There might have been other wardings in place before the lighthouses that have been forgotten. After all, when they were built people didn't think they'd ever be automated. The modern world is always changing. That can make it rough to deal with an ancient threat that stays the same."

Ross seemed to consider his next question for a moment before speaking. "How come it took magic to work the wardings instead of any of the religious organizations?"

For all its reputation as a place for fun and frolic, the state had deep and active religious ties, making their absence notable.

"We don't know for sure that they haven't been involved," Vic pointed out. "Simon talked with Father Anne, and she's working through her channels. All it takes is for an elderly priest to die and not have a successor, and then there's no one to pick up the slack. It would have been easy back in the day to pass a blessing ritual off as asking for protection for the coast in the locations where the lighthouses were later built."

"Okay. Good point. I hope you're right." Ross ran a hand back through his hair and munched a cookie. "I need a break. Totally changing the subject here—at least for a little bit. How's married life working for you?" Ross had been part of Simon and Vic's wedding party and an enthusiastic supporter of their marriage.

"It's not as big of a shift as I expected," Vic confessed. "Maybe it was back in the day when people didn't live together. I already knew that he squeezes the toothpaste tube in the middle and snores when he has a bad cold."

Ross laughed. "Yes, but how about folding towels? Both edges turned inside, or a z-fold? It's the little things that matter."

"Whoever's turn it is to do the laundry gets to pick." Vic pulled a granola bar from his lunch bag, saving the cookie for afterward. "Don't forget, we both lived on our own for years, so we already learned how to keep body and soul together. And since we're both guys, there aren't expectations about whose job it is to do one thing or another."

"I never thought about that," Ross admitted. "Sheila and I figured we were being very progressive making up our own agreements about who did what. And for a lot of stuff, we just take turns. Or whoever is best at it gets stuck with the chore. We learned the hard way that beats making the person who's all thumbs do something they aren't good at."

"Did anything surprise you about being married?" Vic washed down a bite of his bar with coffee.

"At first? How many little things you never think to talk about because you assume everyone does them the way you do, and they don't," Ross said. "What's familiar isn't always what works best. Later on—how good it is when you settle into a rhythm and work together without even thinking about it."

Vic smiled. "Yeah, I like creating our own routines. They might not suit everyone, but they work for us. It's just seamless. Maybe that's part of how you know you got the right one."

Ross rolled his eyes. "As if any idiot couldn't see that both of you besotted fools weren't over the moon for each other."

"Were we that obvious?"

"Ask Cap. Hell, ask the precinct. There was even a betting pool on how long it would take for the two of you to wise up and make it official."

"Seriously?" Vic wasn't sure whether to be horrified or a little flattered.

"It was clear as day to everyone except you two."

They chatted about vacations and the holidays as they finished lunch, and Vic got up to stretch. He dialed Simon, who answered right away.

"Hey, what's up?" Simon asked.

"I think the troll is breaking the truce," Vic told him. Simon remained silent. "Uh, say something?"

"I was going to call you and say the same thing," Simon replied. "Fill me in."

Vic gave him the results from the research he and Ross had done. When he finished, Simon shared what he had learned from Ricky.

"You told me once that supernatural creatures can be picky about the details of agreements," Vic said. "Does that apply to trolls?"

"That's one of the things I've asked Father Anne to look into," Simon replied. "No one does fine print like the fay and the old ones. But even if the troll thinks it found a loophole, that might not automatically work in its favor. And if it has broken the agreement, restoring the lighthouse protections to bind it would be completely legit."

"Are there supernatural lawyers? Because this sounds like stuff we go to court over," Vic asked.

"There are tribunals and barristers—everything tends to have old-fashioned terms," Simon replied. "The good news is that containment in the face of clear harm is a recognized cause to take action, so we don't need permission. That's how monster hunters operate without getting bogged down in the system."

In normal life, Vic wasn't a fan of shoot first, ask questions later. But since joining forces with Simon, he had gained an appreciation for the expediency of frontier justice, at least when it came to the supernatural.

"You know what Ross and I found is probably not the whole picture, right? Without bodies, there's no way to prove that the person isn't still out there somewhere, even though that's highly unlikely. No bones, no DNA," Vic pointed out. "The kinds of places these folks holed up would be perfect for the troll to poof them and not be seen. Hell, even if someone did see them disappear, they either wouldn't tell anyone, wouldn't believe what they saw, or wouldn't be believed even if they did say something."

"I think we've figured out how the troll has co-existed for so long," Simon replied. "As long as he picked victims that the people in charge either didn't value or wanted rid of, the troll didn't get hunted…even without the lighthouse wardings."

"What changed?" Vic asked, although he had a few suspicions.

"Viewpoints. Values. More enlightened approaches became mainstream right about the time the lighthouse wardings weakened. Mental health programs, homeless shelters, intervention services— trying to save people and help them get back on their feet instead of writing them off. That meant a shift from seeing the troll as doing the dirty work of cleaning up problems to viewing it as a monster preying on the most vulnerable people," Simon replied.

"I never thought monsters paid attention to public opinion," Vic replied. He had put the call on speakerphone, and Ross chuckled at his comment.

"Actually, sentient monsters have to pay a lot of attention to the culture around them," Simon said. "Remember all the vampire TV shows where the vamp looks like everyone else, except for not going out during the day? He doesn't swan around in a cape looking like Dracula. Too obvious."

Now that Vic thought about it, all the paranormal shows he had seen lately had vampires, werewolves, and other creatures hiding in plain sight by finding creative ways to blend in. From the people with supernatural abilities Vic had met through Simon, he knew such things were more than just the invention of television scriptwriters.

"And trolls are shapeshifters. So he can look like anyone and change appearance," Simon reminded him. "Keep that in mind. I'm pretty sure the troll knows we're paying attention to him." He told Vic about spotting the tall man just before the traffic signals fell.

"I'm glad you're safe," Vic replied. Ross's eyes had gone wide at the story.

"Yeah, me too."

"Tough to tell if we're being stalked if the troll can change how he looks," Vic observed. "I wonder if the tall man is his main form. Maybe he can't do as much if he's shifted."

"I'll ask Father Anne. That's a good point," Simon replied.

"Like that's not creepy as fuck," Ross muttered.

"Just—be careful," Vic told Simon. "Don't take any crazy chances."

"Same for you," Simon told him. "See you at home."

The cop on desk duty leaned in their doorway. "Hey guys—there's a man here to see you. Are you expecting anyone?"

Vic and Ross exchanged a look. "No, but did he say why he came?"

"He said he was on the force during the gang wars and heard someone was looking into them," the desk cop replied.

"That was over forty years ago," Ross said.

"He's up in years. Should I send him back?"

"Sure," Vic said. "Thank you." The cop returned to the front desk as Vic looked at Ross. "This should be interesting."

Several minutes later the cop escorted an elderly man back to their office.

"I know the way," the man grumbled. "Haven't forgotten everything yet."

"No offense intended, sir," the much younger officer replied, hiding a smile. "Here you are."

The officer looked at Vic and Ross. "This is Mr. Caldwell Henshaw. Mr. Henshaw, Homicide Detectives Vic D'Amato and Ross Hamilton."

"Are you two the ones looking at the gang wars?" the old cop's voice was strong and steady despite his age. He was slight and stooped, but Vic bet from the width of the man's shoulders that he had been a much larger person in his youth.

"Yes, sir." Vic hurried to set out a chair for their guest. "Have a seat, please. How can we help you?"

"Can I get you a cup of coffee?" Ross asked.

The man gave a dismissive wave of his hand. "Thanks, but that just tears up my stomach these days. Guess I overdid it back then." He gratefully accepted a bottle of water and settled into his chair.

"Now, why in the Sam Hill does anyone care about those old fights?" Henshaw demanded after he had taken a swig of water.

Vic and Ross shared a glance. He didn't want to blurt out that they thought a supernatural creature was up to no good, but Vic hadn't come up with a plausible cover story.

"We think that there are certain…interests…who might benefit from the unrest," Vic said, trying to stick as close to the truth as possible. "Play both sides against the middle."

"Ain't there always?" Henshaw said with a sigh. "God, the more things change, the more they stay the same. I thought those cycle gangs got tamed down to be fan clubs where a bunch of desk jockeys dress up and play tough guy."

Vic tried not to snicker since Henshaw's characterization rang true. "I guess that's better for everyone than the alternative. From what I've heard, Myrtle Beach got more family-oriented too, over the years."

"Oh, it's less exciting than it used to be, that's for sure. Can't say that's a bad thing. You boys ever go up to Virginia Beach in your wild days?" Henshaw asked.

Ross raised an eyebrow. "I think I know what you mean. Not exactly the same atmosphere."

Virginia Beach's proximity to several military bases led to a tension between family-friendly entertainment and meeting the interests of horny young men looking for a good time between deployments. While the area had made strides in expanding its appeal to a more general audience, there were still plenty of bars and strip clubs to cater to off-duty interests.

"I've heard," Vic replied. The town of Virginia Beach did its best to be gay friendly, but Vic didn't go looking for trouble, and military bars were trouble with a capital T.

"Myrtle was rough and ready back in the day until the town council teamed up with some bigwig real estate developers to create what's here now," Henshaw said. "Fancy hotels, entertainment venues, concert pavilions, and Ocean Boulevard. It's definitely an improvement over the Wild West."

"So you were on the force during the gang wars?" Ross asked.

"Yep. A whole lot younger than I am today. Bunch of the cycle clubs would get liquored up and pick fights, and then their friends would join in. Next thing you knew, a bunch of them were brawling. Mostly fists, but now and again there would be pipes, chains, brass knuckles, and shots fired. People ended up hurt. There were always several deaths—and more than a few people went missing when the fights were over."

"How do you mean, missing?" Vic asked.

"Just up and disappeared," Henshaw said. "Maybe it's not odd that folks with a drifter lifestyle pick up and leave, but people who earned a place in a club usually stuck around, and in their own rough and tumble way, the members looked out for each other."

"Who reported the missing members?" Ross asked.

"See, that's what always struck me funny because it was someone high up in the clubs that would do it. They'd walk in with a couple of their lieutenants and belly up to the desk and file a missing person report—or three. The day before they'd been swinging punches at each other, and then everything was back to normal."

"Did the cops take the reports seriously?"

Henshaw see-sawed his hand. "Kinda. We didn't think they

were pulling our leg, but we weren't inclined to do extra favors, if you know what I mean."

"What made the club bosses think someone had gone missing as opposed to just taking off on their own?" Ross leaned forward, intrigued.

"Because the bosses were worried. These clubs, they were families. Fucked up, dysfunctional-as-all-hell families, but maybe the best any of their people ever had. They took care of each other, even if they threw punches. And when those bosses came in to file a report, asking us for help when they'd rather gnaw off an arm, I figured they were really worried."

"Did the cops ever find the missing people?" Vic asked.

"Not that I heard."

"Was there anything the missing people had in common?" Ross probed. "Besides being members of the bike clubs?"

Henshaw thought for a moment. "I got the feeling, at the time, that the missing guys were at the bottom of the club's pecking order. They were members, but sort of like the little brother the big kids let hang around. They weren't the muscle guys or the lieutenants or the organizers. They were foot soldiers, glad to have a place to belong.

"Sometimes they were younger, or maybe not as bright, or just clueless. The rest of the club kept an eye on them. So they were upset when the guys went missing, and I think if they ever caught who took them heads would have rolled," Henshaw said.

"There were accusations made, but nothing ever got proved," he continued. "Didn't look like a robbery—the people left all their things behind—including their bikes. Certainly wasn't for ransom. No one said that there were drugs or theft involved. Somebody just turned around and said, 'Where's Fred?' and no one knew."

"People talk," Vic replied. "There are always theories. Did you hear any of the rumors?"

Henshaw shrugged. "This was the eighties. People had theories about everything. UFOs. Bigfoot. The CIA. Some of them were smoking crazy stuff."

"We're pretty open-minded," Ross said. "What did they say about the missing motorcyclists?"

"Well, see, it wasn't just the bikers," Henshaw said. "Back then, Myrtle Beach had a pretty high missing person count. Some got found, others didn't. From what got reported—and that's not going to be everyone who goes missing—I'd have said about eighty to ninety percent eventually got accounted for."

Vic knew that lined up with the national average, allowing for the fact that not all people who went missing were reported or tracked—or wanted to be found.

"But the ones we couldn't find haunted me," Henshaw went on. "I couldn't figure out why them and not others. We didn't find blood or bodies. In most cases, they left all their belongings behind. It was like someone just waved a wand, and poof, they were gone. Sometimes, I still get dreams about that."

"What's your theory? I promise that no matter how wild, we won't laugh," Vic told him.

"Okay, here goes. Don't say I didn't warn you. Ever see one of those sci-fi shows where someone steps into a rift between our world and somewhere else? I don't know what it would take to make that happen—secret government technology, some sort of Russian cyber tech, alien abduction, or real magic—but I think that something unnatural happened to those people."

Henshaw waited for a reaction, and Vic could see the man was braced for ridicule. When they didn't react, he looked from one to the other. "That's it? You don't think I'm nuts?"

Ross shook his head. "Nope. We're just trying to figure out how to fix it."

"I'm not the only one who thought there was something spooky going on," Henshaw said. "There was a lady who claimed to be a witch, hung around with some of the bikers. For a while there, she did a big business in spirit bells. Then the gang wars and the disappearances stopped. Damnedest thing."

Ross and Vic exchanged a look. *Because of the bargain—which the troll is breaking.*

"Was there anything special about the spirit bells the witch made?" Vic asked.

The old man dug into his pocket and pulled out a small steel bell about as wide around as his thumb. It was carved with runes and sigils, some of which Vic recognized from Simon's work and made a pleasant ringing sound.

"I used to ride back in the day. Started out as a motorcycle cop. When I retired, the former head of the club gave me this, said I'd done right by his folks, and wished me well. I didn't ride much after that, but I always hung onto it."

He handed the bell to Vic, who wondered what Simon would make of it.

"I don't know the name of the witch—she might not even be around anymore. But I thought the bell brought me good luck. Now I'm giving it to you, hoping you can figure out how to stop the disappearances once and for all." He grinned and winked.

"Thank you." Vic held the bell in his cupped hand. He felt certain its magic and protections were real. "But don't you still need this?"

"I got it inked a long time ago, just in case." Henshaw pulled up his sleeve to display a perfect replica of both sides of the bell. "This way, I can't lose it." He pushed out of his chair to stand. "Hope you boys can finish what we started."

"We plan to do our best," Ross vowed.

Vic insisted on walking Henshaw to his car, unsurprised that the retired cop had parked in the back, the employee lot. Henshaw gave him a look. "You're not just being nice to an old man. What do you think is out here?"

"We think there's an ancient creature that was held at bay for a very long time by protections that have faded, and it's behind the disappearances. Friends of ours are trying to figure out how to rein it in again."

"I'm guessing that's off the books, unless the police department got a whole lot more exciting since my day," Henshaw said with a knowing look.

"Definitely off the books," Vic replied. "Although our captain knows and supports it."

"Good. There were always strange things that couldn't quite be explained. Even back in my day, there were some guys who took care of that stuff. The rest of us didn't want to know the details, but we were glad they were around." Henshaw gave him a jaunty salute before getting into his Toyota sedan and driving away.

Vic watched the taillights recede and shivered even though the night was warm. He turned in a slow circle, feeling like he was being watched. Half a block away, in the darkness, just outside the street-light's glow, he spotted a tall figure. It was too far to see features, but Vic had the sense the person was staring at him, and it sent a chill down his spine.

He blinked and the man was gone. When Vic came back inside, he heard shouting and swearing. He ran toward the front desk, where he saw several uniformed cops wrestling three clearly inebri-ated men toward the holding cells.

"Book them on drunk and disorderly," the senior officer said. "We'll get their details when they sober up."

"I'm telling you, Don just disappeared!" one of the drunks shouted. "Like in the movies. Gone." He was a wild-looking man in his thirties with a mane of reddish hair, a bushy beard, and he smelled like beer.

"Can you pull him into an interrogation room?" Vic asked the desk cop. "I need to talk to him."

"He's pretty trashed."

"Believe it or not, he's making sense to me, and I don't want him to change his story. I'll have Ross with me. You can run the cameras."

The cop at the desk gave him a dubious look, but did as Vic requested.

"Have a seat," Vic told the drunk, who was handcuffed to the table. "I want to hear about the person who disappeared."

The man suddenly seemed to realize his story could be taken the wrong way. "I didn't do nothin'," he protested. "I swear to god, I didn't make it happen."

Vic held up both hands, palms out, in a gesture of peace. "I believe you. I just want to hear about what you saw. Don't add anything or take anything away. But first, I need to read you your rights."

Once Vic finished with the Miranda warning, he sat across from the drunk. Ross hung out in a corner of the room where he could help if the man got agitated.

"What's your name?"

"Jay."

"Alright, Jay. Who disappeared?"

"My buddy, Don Cutter."

"Can you tell me what Don was doing right before he disappeared?" Vic asked.

Jay looked around nervously. "Am I in trouble?"

"You were brought in for being drunk in public. You aren't in trouble about Don."

"Okay. Look, Don and me, we've been friends for a long, long time. We party together a lot, look out for each other. Know what I mean?" Jay made sense even though his voice had a blur of beer to it.

"We walked outside the club to get some air. We were hanging around the back steps, and Don gets a phone call. He put up a finger to tell me to stick around and walked a few steps away. I'm watching him talk on his phone, and then—poof. He just disappears."

"When you say he disappeared—" Vic started.

"I mean he fuckin' disappeared!" Jay roared. "He was standing there, talking on his phone, and then—beam me up, Scotty—he's gone. I grabbed Jeremy and we walked all around the lot. I thought he might be pranking me, but that wasn't really his style. His phone was right there on the ground, broke the screen when he dropped it. The call was still live. He wouldn't have done that for a joke. You know what phones cost?"

"So you and your friend looked outside—could he have slipped past and gone back into the club?" Vic asked.

Jay ran his free hand through his long, tangled hair. "We looked. Asked everyone. Got the DJ to make an announcement. No one saw him again."

"Did he manage to go home on his own?" Vic didn't believe Don left voluntarily, but he had to explore the options.

"That's where Jeremy and I went next, but he wasn't at his place. We called our friends. No luck."

"Was Don with you all night up to that point? Was he hanging around anyone you didn't know?" Vic asked.

"He was with us. When he went to get a beer, he talked to the bartender and a couple of guys who were at the bar, and then he came back to our gang," Jay replied.

"Was Don going through a rough time?" Vic pressed.

"His mom was real sick, and he just broke up with his girl-friend," Jay said. "We were all trying to cheer him up."

"The guys at the bar, were they still there after Don wasn't?"

Jay thought for a moment. "I wasn't paying them a whole lot of attention, but I think that one of them wasn't around at the end, the tall one. I was focused on finding Don."

"Can you state for the record Don's name, phone number, and address? We'll send a team to check his apartment," Vic requested. Jay complied, and Vic signaled for the recording to stop.

"I'm sorry about your friend," Vic said. "I hope he turns up okay." Vic felt certain that the troll had taken Don. He felt sorry for Jay, who looked truly miserable.

"Come on, let's get you settled so you can sleep it off." Ross walked Jay to his cell.

Vic put in a good word for him on account of his cooperation.

If Simon's theory is right about how often the troll can make someone disappear, this resets the counter to one. Useful to know.

"I'll get Simon to stop by and examine the bell tomorrow," Vic said when he and Ross returned to their office to wrap up for the night. "I'd be surprised if he didn't have some ideas about the witch who made the bell. If she's not still around, she might have a successor."

"Do you think it provided that much protection?"

Vic shrugged. "Maybe. Sometimes little things pack a big punch." They walked out to the parking lot, and he was relieved to catch a glimpse of the protective amulet he had given Ross at the neckline of his shirt.

"Don't forget, I'm off tomorrow. Going to check out lighthouses with Simon to see if we can link his end of the legends and ours."

"Yeah, yeah. Hard day of work cruising up the coast," Ross teased. He grew serious. "Hope you can find something useful. It sounds like whatever pact was in place is gone."

Vic clapped him on the shoulder. "That's the goal. Call me if you need me. And stay clear of the troll."

7

———

SIMON

"Thanks for coming with me." Simon reached over to take Vic's hand as he drove. Much as Vic might have liked the idea of a ride up the coast on his Hayabusa, Simon had argued for the comfort of the car for an all-day outing.

"Sure. It's almost always a great day to take a drive along the ocean." Vic lifted their joined hands and kissed Simon's knuckles. "We've been too damn busy since the wedding to do stuff like this."

They had a beautiful day for the trip, no rain in sight and reasonable temperatures. While they were working the case, Simon vowed to make the day memorable for good reasons and planned to enjoy their investigation as much as possible.

"I've wanted to visit the lighthouses since I moved here," Simon confessed. "I just never took the time."

"We're saving the world. That counts as a priority," Vic joked.

"I thought we'd start with the northernmost lighthouse and work our way south," Simon replied. "The Georgetown Light is still active—one of two still operated by the Coast Guard."

"I guess that improvements in navigational equipment and other technology made some of the lights less useful."

"That and maintaining the lighthouses was expensive—especially when the lighthouse keepers lived on site," Simon said. "Once they figured out how to automate the lights, the job of the keeper went away—at least, the part that the government knew about. Losing the onsite keepers made the supernatural part harder to manage."

Traffic was light, making it easier to drive and have a conversation. A pop station played softly in the background.

"Even being automated, most of the lighthouses aren't still in service," Vic observed. "I'll admit to doing a little homework yesterday to be ready. Two were never even real to start with; they were just built to be pretty."

"We can skip those since they won't have any impact on the magic or the wardings," Simon replied. "Then there's another one that got moved to a golf course once it was deactivated. We won't worry about that one unless we have to."

"Fake lighthouses are disappointing," Vic replied.

"I'm mostly concerned with the two that are still functioning— the Georgetown Light and the Charleston Light—some people refer to it as Sullivan's Island," Simon said. "And the other lights that were once real and operational might still have magical value even though they're decommissioned and dark."

"If there aren't lighthouse keepers anymore—and there won't be again—what's the plan?"

Simon tapped the steering wheel and let out a long breath. "I'll get back to you on that. Still figuring it out. Ideally, I'd like to get volunteers who have some degree of psychic or magical ability to be the keeper of one of the active lighthouses. At least take the mantle for a while and then pass it to someone else."

"Who's going to be in charge of that? It's a bit of a stretch for you to take on." Vic sounded concerned.

"I'm hoping Father Anne and the St. Expeditus Society can oversee it since one of the lighthouses is near Charleston. I think they'd be the best suited."

"That makes sense. You've got the incantation from one of the old keepers. What else do you need to pull this all together and reactivate the protections?" Vic asked.

Simon had grown even fonder of his husband for the way Vic had come to accept Simon's reality.

"I'm still working on the details," Simon replied. "I read the journal from one of the keepers, and it was helpful. But this is the sort of thing where the devil is in the details, and if there was something important that he didn't know about, it would be bad to leave it out by accident."

"How complicated is the incantation? I can't imagine that the Coast Guard recruited highly powerful witches to man the lighthouses."

"Unless there's more to it than what I read in the keeper's journal, middling natural power is sufficient," Simon answered. "Good protections, laid down over and over again, add up to a strong spell layer by layer. The problem comes when the spell isn't reinforced each year. I'm hoping we can turn that around."

The Georgetown Light was the closest to Myrtle Beach and their first stop. It was a white cone with a black top, sturdy and unadorned.

"Looks like it's been here a while," Vic observed.

"Built in 1801, rebuilt several times between storms and the Civil War," Simon explained. "The island used to have homes on it and then a pier and a pavilion for outings. Storms took out the homes, and a fire destroyed the pavilion. Now it's a game preserve. Tourists can't go up in the lighthouse or even land on the island. But I've got tickets for a boat tour that gets as close as we're allowed to go."

The breeze off the ocean made Simon grateful for his light jacket. They parked with time enough to use the restroom and get coffee before the boat left the dock. It was the first trip of the day, and only two other couples were on the tour.

"I've never done a tour like this," Vic yelled over the sound of the boat and the wind. "I always wanted to."

"I wish we had time to do some tours for fun when we go to the Charleston lighthouse."

"Are there any places in Charleston where the tours aren't haunted? I'd like you to actually be relaxed," Vic replied, and

Simon recalled a few times when ghosts had pestered him during an entire tour, trying to correct misinformation from the tour guides.

"Probably not. But that's okay. I'm enough of a history nerd to put up with the ghosts." Standing close to Vic against the wind, Simon closed his eyes and felt the sting of the salt air. The tour guide gave details about the city's history and busy harbor, filling them in as they motored out to the island where the lighthouse stood overlooking the bay. "Maybe we can take a quick trip when the case is over."

"When we get closer to the lighthouse, I'm going to let you listen for anything interesting in the monologue while I try to tune in and see what vibes I get from the lighthouse itself," Simon told Vic.

"If no one is allowed on the island—let alone in the building— how is it going to work to renew the protections?" Vic's voice was barely loud enough to carry above the wind.

"Father Anne and Teag are figuring that out.

The lighthouse loomed large against the blue sky. Simon closed his eyes and sent his psychic feelers in the direction of the structure.

He felt the relentless buffeting of storms and the drench of cold water. Winds howled and waves crashed. He caught glimpses of past keepers and sensed that the ghosts of at least two people, a man and a young girl, still haunted the lighthouse.

He pushed deeper with his senses, beyond the faces and lives of the people who had kept the flame, past the storms and shipwrecks, following a thread of power that illuminated the lighthouse with an old, resilient presence, an essential type of ancient magic.

The thread had grown faint, faded with the deaths of its keepers, but Simon could still make it out, linking the main lights together, protecting residents from storms both physical and supernatural.

He came back to himself with a start. Vic laid a hand on his arm, stilling him and reminding Simon there were other people nearby. Simon nodded in acknowledgment, thinking over what he had sensed as the tour guide continued his storytelling.

When they returned to the pier, Vic tipped the guide and led the way off the boat, keeping close to Simon. "Well?" he asked once the group that had sailed with them dispersed.

"There's still power associated with the light, as well as a couple of faded ghosts," Simon told him. "If it's like that with the other lighthouses, it may be more a matter of restoring the magic than starting over. I think the spells sank deep enough into the land and the structure that they're just waiting for a power boost."

"That would be good, right?"

"It's usually easier to improve something than start over from nothing," Simon replied.

"Next up is Cape Romain." Vic checked the map.

"It's another one you can only get to by boat," Simon told him. "Two brick towers from the mid-1800s. There's a legend that one of the keepers murdered his wife and buried her on the island, and people say you can hear footsteps inside."

The regular tour only went to the island once a month, but Simon had hired a private boat to take them as close as possible.

"It's pretty here." Vic watched a heron take flight. "Lots of birds. Peaceful."

"I wouldn't want to be out here in a bad storm. There's nothing between you and the water." Simon appreciated the view as the boat drew closer. This time, he picked up discordant vibrations.

Simon squirmed in his seat. Vic picked up on the uneasiness immediately. "Talk to me."

"I don't know if the legend about the murder is true, but there are bad vibes. Depression, isolation, instability. I'm guessing more than one of the live-in keepers didn't deal well with being alone. Definitely haunted, and the ghosts are restless," Simon replied.

"Glad we don't have to go up in it. How will that affect a new guardian?"

The brief tour ended, and Simon pushed a windswept lock of hair out of his eyes. They headed back to their car. "That was one of the reasons I wanted to see the lighthouses myself so I could match the guardian with the site. This one needs someone with skill and power. I'm hoping Father Anne has someone from her group in mind."

"Let's go find some grub," Vic said. "Sea air makes me hungry."

Simon felt a shift, and everything went quiet. The light took on an odd reddish glow although it was close to noon. It took him seconds to realize that the world had gone silent around him—no birds singing, waves pounding, or wind rushing past.

He was alone in an empty world, trapped and helpless, doomed. Simon fought back panic, grappling with the nightmare reality of being all alone, forever—

"Simon!" Vic's voice sounded far away, but the edge of panic in it roused Simon from his paralysis. "Simon—wake up!"

Everything shifted again, as if the whole world slid sideways and then righted itself, and Simon blinked, trying to clear his mind. He found Vic only inches in front of him, gripping his shoulders with a panicked expression.

"What happened?" Simon wondered how much time had elapsed.

"Oh, thank God you're back." Vic's fearfulness slid into relief.

"Back?"

Vic's eyes searched his. "What do you remember?"

Simon frowned as he tried to recall the past few minutes and found a blur. "We got in the car to go get lunch. Everything got last man on earth quiet, like there wasn't anyone else on the planet. I knew I was going to die. And then you were shaking my shoulders."

Hearing himself recount the episode made Simon question his sanity, but he feared he knew the explanation.

"Are you okay now?" Vic had gone into cop mode, watchful and wary, using his training to push aside his worry.

"I think so," Simon replied as he did a quick assessment. "I don't smell toast if that's what you mean, and I'm a little young for a stroke. But…"

"What?"

"How long was I out of it? It felt like a minute, tops."

Vic shook his head. "Simon, I've been shaking you and calling your name for at least five minutes, maybe more. You didn't respond. Your eyes were vacant. You were just gone."

Simon felt his heart speed up in response to Vic's worry. "I'm sorry I scared you. Time seemed different to me. I wonder—"

"More of the troll's tricks?" Vic supplied.

Simon nodded. "The lore I found said time distortion along with visions and nightmares."

He knew Vic's expression from working cases together, analytical and focused. "If it's the troll, he didn't strike near the active lighthouse, which supports your theory that the working lights still have mojo," Vic said.

"I think you're right. I'm just not sure yet what to do about it." Simon hadn't missed that blanking out while driving or crossing the street would have been so much worse. "Although I think the amulets and protections are limiting what the troll can do."

"He'll get his strength back soon enough. We're running out of time to figure this out," Vic warned.

Simon took his hand and squeezed it. "I know. And I believe we're going to find the answer."

They stopped for lunch in nearby McClellanville, a tiny town known for its fishing industry. Vic opted for a restaurant that specialized in Cajun-Creole seafood, and they ate outside at a picnic table. The bright sunshine and cool temperatures made it a perfect day. Simon did his best to avoid dwelling on the time distortion incident, and Vic's silence on the issue let him know that his partner was still analyzing what happened.

Next up were the Sullivan Island and Morris Island lights. The Morris Island tower near Folly Beach sat surrounded by water and marshland on a concrete footing, long defunct and deactivated. Simon got a very faint impression from it, barely a glimmer.

Sullivan Island, near Charleston, was still a working light, although no longer manned. Tourists weren't allowed inside, but Simon and Vic got close, and Simon's strong reading of its remaining power encouraged him.

"It's still got a lot of juice," he told Vic. "I think it and Georgetown will be the key anchors for this, with the other lighthouses feeding in."

Hunting Island Lighthouse was a brick tower sheathed in cast iron. Over the decades, it had been relocated farther inland due to encroaching water. Despite looking to be in good condition after a recent renovation, it no longer functioned as a navigational tool. Simon picked up a faint resonance, enough to make him rethink keeping the less powerful lighthouses as part of the protections.

Simon remained alert but didn't have the feeling of being watched. He and Vic added some extra protective charms in their pockets, just in case. He wondered whether the troll had exhausted his magic for the day or if their additional precautions made him draw back.

They stopped for dinner in Beaufort, another coastal town famous for its history, tourist attractions, and restaurants. The town was also known for its joking feud with Beaufort, NC, since while the towns were spelled the same, they were pronounced differently.

"North Carolina says 'bow-fort,'" Simon told Vic. "Down here, we say 'bew-fort.' It's an easy way to tell who's from out of town."

"Pittsburgh has the same kinds of things," Vic replied, remembering his hometown. "Some of the river names are real tongue-twisters, like Monongahela and Youghiogheny. Or whether those potato-filled dumplings are pronounced 'pi-ro-hee' or 'pi-ro-gee.'"

They treated themselves to a fancier restaurant with a water view. Since they were driving, they skipped the wine, agreeing to have a toast when they got home. Simon got crab bisque and fried oysters with a tall glass of iced tea. Vic ordered shrimp and grits with an iced coffee.

"I don't think the other lighthouses are going to factor into the protections," Simon told Vic as they ate. "The Governor's Lighthouse and the Harbour Town Lighthouse were built as tourist attractions and never were actual working navigational lights. Haig Point was a private beacon, not a full Coast Guard lighthouse, and it's now a hotel."

"That's creative." Vic dug into the grits with gusto.

"The Bloody Point Lighthouse got turned into a private home. And the Leamington Lighthouse—said to be haunted—was moved inland, and now it's on a golf course." Simon finished his soup, which was excellent, before moving on to the oysters.

"I'm hoping that we can do what needs to be done without either Bloody Point or Leamington because there would be ongoing problems with access," Simon pointed out. "I'm supposed to talk with Father Anne tomorrow to see what she's come up with."

They finished the meal with large slices of Key Lime pie and tall coffees for the road. The sunset over the ocean was a beautiful ending to the day, which, while it had been primarily research, offered a long-overdue couples' day out as well.

Simon couldn't resist turning up the radio on a Top 40 channel and putting the windows down as they drove.

"I feel like I'm in a road trip movie." Vic rested his arm on the door and let the breeze ruffle his dark hair.

Simon's man bun kept his long hair out of his eyes. "Works for me. Once we fix this lighthouse mess, we're going to need another vacation to de-stress."

The drive home didn't seem to take long as they sang along with the music and talked about the highlights of the day. When they finally arrived at the blue bungalow, Simon leaned over to kiss Vic before they got out of the car.

"Thanks for going with me. Even research is better when we're together."

Vic kissed him back. "I like having a better understanding of what you're doing and how you think. So much of it is still new to me, but I'm learning."

"You're a quick study." Simon paused as he reached for the door handle.

"Something wrong?" Vic immediately moved into cop mode.

"Validating that whenever we were close to one of the working lighthouses, the feeling of being watched went away," Simon replied. "It's back again."

"That wouldn't surprise me." Vic got out of the car and walked around to Simon's side like a security detail to accompany him into the house. "Didn't you tell me that power can sink into the land itself and the bones of a structure?"

"Glad to know you're listening."

Vic stayed alert, watching their surroundings as he unlocked the door.

"And you're right—it can sink in," Simon said. "But without

being renewed and strengthened, I suspect that the range gets smaller and smaller. Instead of protecting the whole coast and keeping the troll constrained, the power is in a more limited area around the lighthouses."

They turned on lights, clicked the television to life, and checked to ensure nothing was amiss. Simon believed that the wards he had placed around the house and shop were strong enough to hold against most attacks, but he had never gone up against a troll and didn't want to push his luck.

When he returned to the living room, Vic poured glasses of wine. They settled onto the couch and turned on the end of a sci-fi movie they had seen a dozen times.

Simon slipped his arm around Vic's shoulders, and Vic leaned into his side. "Next time, let's go up the coast and see stuff that isn't haunted," Simon suggested.

"Do places like that exist?"

"Yeah, but not in the historic tourist areas—which are interesting because they're old. The deeper the history, the more ghosts," Simon replied. "Of course, even in places we consider relatively new, there were always people before us, and they had their own stories and ghosts."

"So everywhere is haunted, and we're tripping over ghosts everywhere we go."

"Pretty much."

Now that they were off the road and safe at home, Simon felt the effect of driving all day, especially after drinking a glass of wine. "I'm all for sexy times in the morning, but I'm fading fast," he told Vic after they had exchanged heated kisses. "Rain check?"

Vic laughed and kissed him on the nose. "Gonna give me blue balls," he teased. "But I'm not surprised between the driving and being outside all day. Let's lock up and cuddle tonight, and we can go at it like sex-crazed ferrets in the morning."

Simon drew back and gave Vic a skeptical look. "Okay, not the most romantic image, but—"

"Just wanted to see if you were paying attention." Vic laughed.

They carried their goblets to the kitchen. Vic turned off the lights while Simon again checked the doors and wardings.

"Come on, it's time for bed." Vic held out his hand for Simon and gave him a kiss.

It didn't take either of them long to get changed and through the bathroom. Simon pulled Vic against him in bed, loving the way they fit together. "Sweet dreams," Simon murmured, already starting to drift off. "Looking forward to sexy times in the morning."

Simon stood on the small pad of concrete that surrounded the Morris Island Lighthouse. The sea loomed just a few feet away, deep and cold.

When it was built, the lighthouse had been reasonably inland, but storms gradually left the tower surrounded by water. The wind buffeted Simon, and he shivered.

"You know what you need to do," a ghostly voice whispered. "Bring us back to fight the danger."

"I'm planning to," Simon told the disembodied voice. "A lot has been forgotten."

"Remember us, and we will do our duty. We swore a vow that did not end with death."

Simon woke with a start. Vic mumbled and turned over but didn't rouse.

I need to see if I can summon the ghosts of the guardians to help. They might not all answer, but if some of them lend their assistance, it will strengthen the new wards.

The next morning, a leisurely round of sixty-nine followed by slow, lingering love-making was well worth the wait. Simon and Vic showered together, not quite ready for round three, but with promises to pick up where they left off once Vic got home from work.

After Vic headed for the station, Simon set his laptop on the kitchen table and pulled up an ensorcelled encrypted video meeting program right in time for his appointment. One by one, Father Anne, Gabriella, and Miss Eppie flickered into view.

"Good morning, everyone! Nice to see you all," Simon greeted them, raising his coffee cup in a toast.

"Good morning to you, Sebastian," Miss Eppie replied. "And to everyone."

"Same," Father Anne chimed in. "It's been a hot minute."

"I swear every day goes faster than the one before it." Gabriella shook her head.

"Vic and I drove to the South Carolina lighthouses—at least to the ones most likely to have any protective mojo left." Simon gave them a quick recap of their adventure, relating which sites he thought were their best bets for any spellcasting and renewed wardings and which had minimal or no power remaining.

"Well, first off, I envy you the drive," Father Anne admitted. "It sounds like fun. I hope you got to enjoy yourselves at least a little."

"There are some mighty fine places to eat on that stretch," Miss Eppie pointed out. "The view is fantastic, but the crab cakes are even better."

"Yes to all that," Gabriella replied. "And now I'm hungry!"

They all laughed, easing the tension that went with the subject matter.

"I looked over the notes and photos you sent me from the lighthouse keeper's journal." Father Anne eased into the main topic. "And I found someone who was a direct descendent of the Charleston light's keeper, who was able to corroborate. So I'm feeling pretty good about the incantation and the general outline of the protections."

"Four lighthouses that were once operational are now either tourist attractions, converted to houses, or defunct," Simon added. "Three of them would have access problems if we needed to make regular visits to maintain new wardings. There is a faint hint of energy left on the fourth, but I didn't know if we needed to include it since the other lighthouses are stronger."

"Teag Logan has been going over the information you've sent him from Vic and Ross," Father Anne said. "He agrees that it's likely the troll has been breaking the bargain with the motorcycle gang for quite a while, focusing on taking people who won't be missed. That means the entity won't be as weakened as he might have been, so we need to be braced for a more formidable foe. He won't like being on a diet."

"Damn," Simon muttered under his breath. He hadn't doubted Vic's research, but this was one time when he had hoped Teag would find a flaw in the data.

"I want to reach out to the ghosts of the lighthouse keepers," Simon added. "One of them contacted me and wanted to be involved. I think for some of them, the protective wardings were considered almost a holy obligation."

"That makes sense," Father Anne agreed. "Even though most of the keepers had families, it was a semi-monastic life, and it took a person with a highly protective nature to deal with the hardships."

"I can't imagine how it was in the days before phones and computers," Miss Eppie said. "They might have had radios and telegraphs, but they didn't get back to shore often. I imagine they read a whole lot of books."

"It raises the question of whether someone in the know chose keepers who had at least some supernatural abilities," Simon mused. "They also needed to be open-minded enough to be willing to work the protective wardings and not freak out over it being magic."

"Oh, I imagine a bit of psychic know-how went into it," Gabriella agreed. "Certainly didn't end up that way by accident. It also meant that someone at the Coast Guard must have known, since they were in charge of the lighthouses."

"Technology and cost-cutting led to automating the locations, but I wonder if a change in the people in charge also meant that the new bosses either didn't know or didn't believe in the supernatural protections, so they weren't worried about what happened when there wasn't anyone to carry on," Simon replied.

"Wouldn't be the first time." Miss Eppie sighed.

"I turned a couple of our scholars loose on the St. Expeditus library, which has information from all over the world. They're looking at lore about trolls. Apparently the most common way of dealing with them was warded lighthouses if the creatures were near the ocean, or beacons if those monsters were in mountainous areas," Father Anne added. "Particularly in Europe, they often solved the continuity problem by making the locations into monasteries. Elsewhere, the sites were usually maintained by ascetics or meditative communes who saw it as part of their debt to society."

"Which would make continuity less of a problem because an outside third party wasn't going to suddenly decommission the location," Simon noted.

"Exactly," Father Anne replied.

"How about you, Miss Eppie, Gabriella?" Simon asked.

"I'm particularly interested in the Morris Island light," Miss Eppie replied. "Back during the Civil War, runaway slaves found shelter on the island. I don't doubt that a creature like a troll took advantage of people who were so vulnerable. We might find that their ghosts choose to be allies in some way when they know what's at stake."

"What do we need to work the ritual? Because the troll has figured out something is going on. Vic and I dodged a few strange things that could have been weirdly random—or the troll giving a warning even if our protections keep him from directly harming us."

They listened as he told them about the incidents, wondering whether they would agree it was the troll or his imagination.

"I don't think you can afford to see that as anything other than attacks," Gabriella said. "The troll either didn't have the power—right then—to do real harm, or he didn't choose to, for some reason. But he's reminding you that he knows you're onto him and warning you to back off."

"Even if we did step back—which I've got no intention of doing—it wouldn't stop the troll from making me disappear when he powered back up to eliminate the threat," Simon pointed out.

"True," Miss Eppie agreed. "I don't think you dare ease up. If we can bind the troll, we can save a lot of lives."

"We have a solid version of the incantation, and I've put together a ritual warding ceremony that I think will be strong enough to last for at least a year at a time," Father Anne replied.

"It's also simple enough and not too weird if anyone happens to notice what we're doing."

"No eye of newt and tongue of frog?" Gabriella joked.

"Fortunately not," Father Anne said. "Now we just have to come up with the right people."

"I'm going to talk to a couple of my Skeleton Crew," Simon told them. "I think they have enough ability and experience to help with the wardings, even if they don't become the keepers. We're going to need guardians for the Georgetown and Sullivan's Islands lights who have more power and occult know-how because they're the strongest focal places."

"St. Expeditus can staff the guardians and ensure the lighthouses are handled going forward," Father Anne said. "That keeps continuity and a central point of contact to ensure the ceremony is done right."

"Thank you." Simon, Miss Eppie, and Gabriella all spoke at the same time.

"You're very welcome. Having said that, there's strength in numbers," Father Anne replied. "Teag is talking to the supernatural community in Charleston to see if there are any of the witches and psychics who want to help. We've also got a necromancer, so any of the ghosts of the lighthouse keepers who want to continue to be part of it are welcome."

"We have people from Voudon plus brujas and curanderos who will add their power," Gabriella said, and Miss Eppie nodded.

"I can gather the ghosts who want to maintain their oaths." Simon paused to take a drink of coffee. "I'm going to reach out to the folks at St. Cyprian University. What about the descendants of the keepers?"

Miss Eppie shrugged. "If they want to help, the more the merrier. Having vestigial energy from the original guardians should strengthen the working."

"I agree," Father Anne said. "Our people will be doing the magic, speaking the incantation, and working the spell. Having sympathetic psychic energy surrounding us will lend us power and help protect us when we're vulnerable. The troll isn't going to want to be reined in."

"When we're done, does it void the deal with the motorcycle club?" Simon knew that many of the sacrificed members went willingly, but he still hated the idea of a blood offering.

"It should," Father Anne replied. "From everything I've found, yes. Because we're going to bind the troll by the guardian magic to stop him from preying on humans—all humans."

"What happens then?" Miss Eppie asked. "He starves?"

"Not likely," Gabriella spoke up. "There are animals and fish. He can sustain himself. But he will be weakened, and feeding from sources like that won't strengthen his magic."

"Correct," Father Anne confirmed. "That squares with what we've been able to find from the St. Expeditus archive and European lore. I'm pleased to hear it validated from other magical legacies."

Miss Eppie's root work drew from African sources, while Gabriella tapped traditions from Central and South America as well as Mexico.

"What about logistics? Other than the guardians, is there a benefit to having people physically present at the locations when we do the ritual? Because for several of the spots, it's going to be a stretch just to get one person close enough," Simon asked.

"I've been thinking about that," Father Anne replied. "I think if you set up a group in Myrtle Beach and we have another group here in Charleston, we should be able to focus and concentrate the energy. We'll be closest to the two most powerful lighthouses—Georgetown and Sullivan's Island, and not far from the remaining, lesser lights. I can ask Teag if he's got any contacts down in the Hilton Head area who could hold space for us, but those lighthouses aren't really part of what we're doing."

"How about the North Carolina lighthouses?" Miss Eppie asked. "Wasn't there a seven-pointed star connecting them?"

"It works for those locations, and it's a nice well of power, but the South Carolina lighthouses are in a line down the coast, so that's not a thing we can recreate," Father Anne replied.

"How soon can we do this? The troll's attacks are happening more often." Simon reminded them.

"The full moon is in two days," Father Anne pointed out. "My folks at St. Expeditus are already on standby, so it's really how quickly you can marshal your folks to lend support."

"We know the troll just took another person, so that timing should work for us to be in his recharge cycle," Simon told them. "I'd rather do it sooner than later because we don't know how long it takes for him to power back up."

The supernatural community had its own informal grapevine, and those on the call were well-connected, so spreading the request wouldn't take long.

"I'm happy to have people gather at my shop since we can't take a crowd close to the Georgetown Lighthouse," Simon volunteered. "My Skeleton Crew are comfortable at the store, and ghosts don't take up much space. But I feel like I need to be with the group going to Georgetown. And that means Vic will be with me."

"Eppie and I will go with you," Gabriella offered. "I agree, Simon, that you should be near one of the powerful lighthouses. I have a very strong reading on that."

Miss Eppie nodded. "So do I. Go. We'll make sure there are associates who can handle both the living and the dead at the shop."

"I'll let Cassidy and Teag and the Charleston contingent know," Father Anne said. "May wardings and light protect us all."

They talked logistics for a few more minutes, then ended the call. Simon felt a little better about the plan, although he knew it was still an enormous risk. His stomach growled, and he decided to set the planning aside and eat lunch.

Simon warmed a plate of leftovers and checked to make sure Vic hadn't been trying to reach him. Then he headed into the shop, where Pete had already opened for business.

"Hey, boss! Everything okay?" Pete greeted as he rang out a customer.

Once Simon knew they were alone, he gave Pete as quick an update as he could.

"Wow. That's some story. Whoever said that truth was stranger than fiction didn't know the half of it," Pete said.

"Since the working is just a couple of days away, would you and Mikki be willing to continue staying upstairs? You'll be safer there. Gabriella will have some of her people helping with the gathering here, so you don't have to be involved unless you want to be."

"We can hang a closed for a private event sign on the door to keep out looky-loos," Pete suggested. "Because it's definitely an invitation-only party."

"That's perfect. Please clear my calendar that day too. I'm sorry to have to reschedule people, but I have a feeling all hell is going to break loose," Simon replied.

"Already planning to. Any time afterward will be good, right? Either the troll will be managed, or we'll be in too much deep shit to care."

"I don't know that I would have put it that way exactly, but you've got the gist of it. I don't think the troll will be happy with us, and if he still has the mojo to strike back, it's not going to be pretty," Simon answered.

"Can you actually destroy the troll, or just cut down on how much damage he can do?" Pete asked, and Simon was proud that his assistant seemed nonplussed at the idea of a major magical gathering downstairs from his temporary apartment.

"I don't think it's possible to destroy him—from what we've figured out, he's an ancient, elemental creature. But we should be able to rein him in, which is what the original guardian wardings did," Simon replied.

"I guess the people who set up the protections with the lighthouse keepers never envisioned a time when the lights wouldn't be manned and the guardians would die out. And without a central group overseeing the magic—like the St. Expeditus folks will be doing from now on—there was no one to organize a Plan B."

"It's funny, we hear so much about shipwrecks and pirates, and I'm sure there was plenty of drama on top of the legends," Pete said, "But beyond isolation, no one ever thinks about the lighthouses and their keepers. On bad days, I think being off on an island by myself would be sorta nice."

Simon laughed. "Oh, I totally understand, although I'd take Vic with me. But not dealing with the hustle and bustle of everything and getting paid for it? Sounds amazing."

"Although I might change my mind in a hurricane," Pete mused. "The keeper had to stay at his post to man the light, even in the worst weather. Which I'm sure was absolutely terrifying. Not the kind of thing you want to have a front-row seat to watch."

"And those stairs would be hard on the knees. I wouldn't want to go up and down them all the time. Then again, it was built-in cardio since many of the lights didn't have much open space around them," Simon pointed out.

"Have you figured out what you're reading for the Halloween program at the library?" Pete asked, switching subjects. "Any new inspirations from real life?"

"I don't think 'the troll that poofed Myrtle Beach' would be a bestseller," Simon replied, laughing. "I think I might see if I can find books about lighthouses for both kids and adults. I'd love to see if one of the keepers from any of the Carolina lights wrote either true stories or fiction about it."

"Bonus points if it's either a haunted lighthouse or involves a ghostly pirate or shipwreck," Pete said.

"Sounds reasonable to me." Despite the troll and the threat of catastrophe, planning a library event was a sure way to brighten Simon's day.

"Go do what you need to do," Pete told him. "I've got things covered here."

Simon felt the boardwalk calling to him. "I think I need to take a walk to clear my head. Want me to bring anything back for you?"

"If you're getting coffee, I won't turn down a large pumpkin spiced anything."

"Almost like you read my mind. I haven't seen Tracey much since we got back from our honeymoon, and I owe her an update."

Tracey Cullen owned Le Mizzenmast—usually called Le Miz— which Simon believed sold the best coffee on the Grand Strand. She was one of the people he had known the longest since he moved to Myrtle Beach, and next to Vic and Pete, his closest friend.

"Tell her hi for me," Pete said.

Simon stepped out onto the boardwalk. His thoughts seemed jumbled and noisy, and he could feel a headache coming on. He knew that they had a great team working together on the project, people who were both knowledgeable about the arcane and had strong supernatural gifts. But no one had first-hand experience with trolls, and the stakes were too high to risk making a mistake.

He found an empty bench facing the ocean and sat, staring at the waves and trying to calm his mind. The beachgoers were older couples and retirees since kids and college students were back at school. Out of the corner of his eye, he sensed the ghosts from all eras who had never left the shore or were drawn to walk along the edges of the waves until they were ready to move on.

"I believe you are doing the right thing."

Simon tried not to visibly react when Sister Petroula's ghost showed up seated next to him. He fought the urge to reply aloud.

"You heard all that?"

"I heard enough. It is a terrible thing that the guardians died out, and the keepers were not replaced. People who don't understand the power of magic end up paying its price," the ghost replied.

"Did you mean that trying to renew the protections was the right thing or that our approach is correct? Because no one's done this before."

"Both, so far as I know. After you left, I followed the trail of your research. You were thorough. I did not find any sources you missed. Everything that was been done can be done again. The original protections were put into place. They can be renewed or replaced. Your work appears to be correct," Sister Petroula's spirit answered.

"Thank you. I hope we're both right. Because we can't afford to be wrong."

8

VIC

"Whatever's going down, we want to be part of it." Chad Samuels from the Low Rangers Motorcycle Club strode into the office Vic shared with Ross. He was a big man, probably six foot, five inches, with broad shoulders and tattooed, muscular arms. Even though gray peppered his dark, curly mane and beard, he looked like he could go a few rounds with just about anyone and come out on top.

"I was Carter's top lieutenant, and now I'm in charge. This was our fight first—and we want to finish it."

Vic blinked. "What do you mean?"

Samuels fixed him with a glare. " The curse. The deal. Whatever that *thing* is that's been taking my people. I hear you've been asking questions, and so has that professor who talks to ghosts down on the boardwalk. This has been a plague on us for decades, and if there's a way to make it stop, me and my boys want in."

"I thought your folks had made peace with the situation," Ross said in a dry tone.

"When you think you don't have choices, you make the best of it," Samuels retorted. "When you find out there's an option, things change." He had a whisky rasp to his voice and smelled like Marlboros.

Vic looked to Ross, who shrugged.

"The plans are still coming together. I'll give you the overview. If you still want in, there's a place for you. If not, all I ask is don't get in our way." Vic gestured for Samuels to have a seat.

"That's fair."

Vic walked him through the discovery of the creature's identity, how ancient he was, the role of the lighthouses, and how they had helped to constrain the troll.

"Once the lighthouses weren't manned anymore, the protections faded, and the troll ran amok. He's been cheating on your deal by snatching homeless folks that don't get counted," Vic said. "We've found a way to renew the power of the lighthouses that should bring the creature to heel—and break your club's deal."

Samuels looked at him. "A troll. They're real?"

"Apparently so. Ancient—as in, he was here before the pilgrims came. There are tales about a being like that in the lore of the native tribes along the coast. The tribes say he was already here when *they* first arrived. For all we know he woke when the continent rose," Vic replied.

"You keep saying protections and wardings—you're talking about some sort of magic, aren't you?" Samuels cocked his head and gave Vic a knowing look.

Vic nodded. "Yes. As well as ghosts and people with paranormal abilities."

"Well, fuck. Hot damn."

Ross looked bemused. "You're taking this pretty well."

"My club's been sacrificing to a monster. I've got demon bells on my bike and tats to ward off evil, and my lady runs the club coven. I don't understand how supernatural shit works, but I know it's real."

Vic let out a relieved breath. Having Samuels on board with the concept made things easier.

"I'll let Simon—the professor on the boardwalk—know," Vic said. "If your coven wants to play a role, I can get them in touch with him. We believe the troll will try to strike back and stop the ritual. So if the club is willing to provide security, we could use the help. As I understand it, we need some people at the lighthouses, at the shop where some of the witches will be sending us power, and at the homeless shelters."

"The shelters?" Samuels raised an eyebrow.

"The troll has been poaching unhoused people, and if he feels under attack and has enough energy, he might gobble up more than usual for the power boost," Ross said. "We're trying to spread the word that there have been attacks, so people are safer in the shelters."

"I can see that," Samuels agreed. "But my folks can't fight a troll. If we could, we'd have never agreed to that stupid deal."

"You can hold a protective line if our friends provide the wardings," Vic said. "We can show you how."

Samuels nodded. "Okay. We can do that. And I'll ask my lady if the coven would help. If she says yes, I'll put her in touch." He rose and extended his hand. Vic gave a firm shake.

"If this gets us out of that damn deal, you've done us a solid. We will remember," Samuels told him before he turned and left.

Vic looked to Ross. "Well, that spared me an awkward phone call." He went to refill his coffee. "I needed to ask for their help, and I wasn't sure that would go well. I'm glad they're on our side—at least for this."

"Strange bedfellows and all that," Ross agreed. "We will need to come up with a caution statement for the shelters that gets attention without starting a Grand Strand serial killer rumor."

"I'm working on it." Vic returned to his desk. "I think we can work with threats, reports, and sources. As in, reports from sources that have documented threats against people living on the streets. We are recommending that those without housing go to shelters until the danger is past."

"Wow—you're good at saying something without actually saying anything," Ross joked. Vic threw a wad of paper at him.

"It's a gift. Except it never worked on my mother."

"We ought to run it by Cap, just in case," Ross said. "It's vague enough I can't see him having a problem with it, and that should keep the media from swooping in looking for a spree killer."

"That was my thought," Vic agreed. "This is coming together fast. If we can get his buy-in this afternoon, we can put out a notice to the agencies by end of day. That gives them tomorrow to pull folks in and get them settled before the shit hits the fan."

"I assume when this goes down, you're going to be with Simon at the lighthouses?" Ross didn't make it a question.

Vic sobered quickly and took a sip of the hot, strong coffee before he answered. "It's where I need to be. Someone has to watch his back—and pull him back from the brink, if it comes to that. He can lose track in the moment and go all-in."

"Yeah, you have that in common." Ross raised an eyebrow.

"I admit it. And he's had my six when I needed it. Goes with the rings." Vic raised his left hand and wiggled the fingers. He spent the next half-hour drafting and refining the notice to the homeless organizations before passing it to Ross for his opinion. Then Vic printed a copy and went to speak with the captain.

"I've heard rumors that people were disappearing under the radar," Hargrove said after he had read the paper. "Nothing official, but people who have an outreach to those folks have been concerned for a while. Of course, if you can't document names and places, there's nothing the cops can do."

"We believe the creature is smart enough to find the most vulnerable people—the chronically unsheltered—and go after them as easy pickin's," Vic replied. "I hate smart monsters, human or otherwise."

"Amen, brother," Hargrove muttered. "I like how you worded this, so it's a warning without setting off a major panic and landing on the six o'clock news."

"That's the goal," Vic said. "If we release this to the specific agencies involved, it will at least buy some time, maybe, before a news van shows up and they give the killer a hashtag."

Hargrove passed a hand over his eyes. "Oh, God. Just shoot me now." He handed the paper back to Vic. "I assume there's a plan?"

"Working on it."

"Do I want to know?"

"Would you prefer plausible deniability?" Vic asked, only partly joking.

"Will it involve explosions?"

"Hopefully not."

"Do you think the media will catch wind of it? Because there's nothing they can't turn into a panic," Hargrove grumbled.

"I think we can spin it as a New Age Wiccan Halloween blessing if anyone asks," Vic answered. "With motorcycle gang escort."

"You're going." Hargrove didn't even make it a question.

"Gotta watch over my guy." Vic shrugged. "Because he's got the self-preservation instincts of a brave dodo. He'll get busy saving the world and forget to live through it unless he's got me."

"That would be a great loss. Just do me a favor—try to stay low visibility. I don't want to explain to the City Council."

Vic grinned. "I can handle that."

Hargrove met his gaze. "You think this will work?"

Vic sobered. "I sure as hell hope so. Simon's got a pretty powerful coalition. And we know the troll was bound before. If they could do it back then, we can do it now. I hope."

"I like the part about using the motorcycle club for security," Hargrove said. "They've got skin in the game, and if the creature has accomplices, they'll think twice after they see the backup."

Vic was amused that the captain didn't bring himself to say troll but knew better than to make a comment.

"It's the same reason I'm going along with Simon, even though I've got zero magic. When the witches are deep into concentrating on raising the power and directing it toward what they need to do, they can't pay attention to what's around them. Despite all that magic, they're vulnerable," Vic explained. "It's really not like in the movies."

"Be careful," Hargrove said in a gruff tone. "I don't have time to recruit a replacement."

Vic took that as the benediction it was meant to be. "Yes, sir."

When he got back to the office, Ross made a shooing motion.

"Go home. I'll finish up. Spend some time with your boy before the big showdown. I'll see you tomorrow."

Vic gave him a wave and a grateful salute, grabbed his messenger bag, and slipped out the door.

Simon wouldn't be home yet, so Vic stopped to pick up some extra outdoor light strings for the bungalow's Halloween decorations and called ahead to order dinner so neither of them had to cook. While he walked through the seasonal aisle at the home improvement store, he also spotted a cute Christmas gnome.

"For luck," he muttered to himself as he tossed it into his basket. Buying a Christmas decoration assumed they would both be here to deck the halls.

Vic had grown up around cops and knew they all had their rituals and superstitions. Since learning more about the supernatural from Simon, Vic came to realize that those protective patterns had some home-spun magic to them and were more than just feel-good busywork.

He hoped the gnome counted.

Simon and I just got married. I want us both to live to a ripe old age and not get sucked into a vortex. Or poofed by a troll.

Vic still beat Simon back home. He set the light strings on top of the box of other decorations that took up space in the dining room and put the bag of Thai food in the middle of the kitchen table, wrapped in dish towels to stay warm.

Just as Vic finished setting out the plates and silverware, Simon arrived. He swept Vic into his arms for a kiss, and held on just a little longer than usual, pressed tight.

"I love coming home to you." Simon pressed in for another kiss. "And you picked up dinner?"

Vic reluctantly let go. "Figured there was enough going on; someone else could cook."

"There are so many reasons I love you." Simon's voice sounded teasing, but Vic read the emotions in his eyes.

He's just as worried as I am over everything. We're both whistling in the dark.

"Go ahead and sit down. Everything's ready." Vic set out glasses of water. "I stopped at the store on the way home, so we have enough lights to decorate."

"And you randomly picked up a good luck holiday gnome?" Simon raised an eyebrow, and Vic knew he was busted.

"Figured it couldn't hurt." He turned away, knowing that Simon probably understood far too well.

"Talk to me." Simon confirmed Vic's guess. "Is this about the lighthouse gathering?"

Vic shrugged. "It's about me wanting to keep you safe, even though this is a threat that's way above my pay grade. So I'm going to do what I can do and hope it's enough."

"I don't want you to get hurt." Simon turned to take Vic into his arms. "Once I'm caught up in the incantation, it's going to be my whole focus. I feel like I'm leaving you vulnerable."

"That's why you need someone watching your back," Vic reminded him. "Because you do lose track of everything, and I can make sure the troll doesn't take advantage of that."

"You're crazy and brave, and I love you." Simon leaned in to kiss Vic. "Which is also why I'm afraid to risk you."

Vic kissed him back, taking control, trying to say with his body what he didn't always find words to express. *I need you. You mean everything to me. I can't lose you.*

"If something goes wrong, I want to be there to put it right," Vic told him. "If something comes after you, I intend to stop it. What you're doing is going to save hundreds of lives. But mostly, it's because wherever you are, that's where I want to be. *Wherever.*"

He let the emphasis make it clear to Simon that included the Valley of the Shadow.

"I don't think it's going to come to that," Simon replied, all playfulness gone from his voice. "If I did, I'd fight harder to keep you away."

"If you tried, I'd still follow." Vic lifted a hand to trail his fingers down the side of Simon's face. "And I hope it doesn't come to that. But whatever happens, I'll have your back."

They separated reluctantly, realizing the food was getting cold.

After the seriousness of the last discussion, conversation lagged as they ate until Vic spoke up.

"The new leader of the Low Rangers who took over for Carter Edwards is totally on board with them being security for the homeless shelters, the store, and anywhere else you need them. They have a lot of members, so that gives you some backup."

"He was okay with everything?" Simon looked as surprised as Vic had felt.

"Turns out he's married to the witch who heads up the club's coven. Who knew, right?" Vic told him. "He's going to ask her if the coven will lend support so you could end up with more witches."

Simon looked surprised. "Wow. I had no idea. That would be great. We need all the help we can get."

After dinner, Vic found an empty corner for the gnome while Simon added the new light strings to what they had already hung. They would wait to put up the big inflatable dragon until trick-or-treat night.

"I can't believe it's almost Halloween," Vic said. "Not just on account of the lighthouse situation, but how fast the year has gone. It always feels like we barely get the pumpkins taken down when it's time to put up the Christmas tree." He couldn't help crossing his fingers that nothing would derail their holiday plans.

"Hey, let's not lose the time we have right now worrying about the future." Simon's voice cut through Vic's worries, especially when Simon went to his knees right there in the kitchen and pressed his face against Vic's groin.

"I like your idea of a distraction." Vic's heartbeat sped up as Simon mouthed along the denim before flipping his button open and easing the zipper down. "Very…effective."

"Must not be." Simon pressed his lips against Vic's briefs. "You're still talking."

Vic caught his breath as Simon shoved jeans and briefs down in one move, and his already-hard cock sprang to attention. Simon nuzzled Vic's package, and then kisses turned to licking before he swallowed him down as far as he could.

"Oh, fuck," Vic gasped, gripping Simon's shoulders as Simon bobbed and licked enthusiastically. "So good."

Vic was getting close, and Simon slipped his hand beneath Vic's balls, fondling them and teasing his taint.

Vic came, shouting Simon's name, bucking against his mouth and grinding into his hand. Simon rode it out with him, swallowing as much as he could and licking Vic through the aftershocks when he finished.

"Oh, God. That was—"

Simon chuckled. "Glad you enjoyed it." He pulled off his T-shirt to clean them off before tucking Vic back into his jeans.

"I want to return the favor," Vic growled.

"Too late. I already came. Now I'm sticky." Simon rose, grimaced at the wet spot in his underwear, and leaned in to give Vic a kiss. "Shower with me?"

Vic happily agreed, and they took their time under the warm water, rubbing out knots in sore shoulders and touching all over until they were both hard again. This time, Vic took their cocks in hand and worked them to release.

"Best dessert ever," Simon sighed as they dried off, sated and warm.

They slipped under the sheets, pressing close together in bed. Vic wrapped his arms around Simon protectively. *We'll figure this out. I'll keep you safe. Somehow.*

That night, Vic's dreams were dark, but inside the heavily warded house where the troll couldn't reach, he knew they were fed not by magic but by his own misgivings. He startled awake, although Simon didn't stir.

They're just dreams. Not even projections from the troll. My imagination and fears running wild.

Not a prophecy or a sending. Not fated or pre-ordained. We can change it. Stop the troll. Save people, and protect Simon.

All we need is some magic—and a little luck.

The next morning, after a repeat of the previous night's sexy times, Vic reluctantly left for the office.

"Keep me posted," he told Simon. "And don't get second thoughts about sneaking off without me. I'm going with you. End of story, period, that's all she wrote."

Simon chuckled despite the serious topic. "Okay. I get it. Together forever. And…thank you. Love you—stay safe."

"You too." Vic forced himself not to turn around before he got to the Hayabusa and roared away. He made sure his guardian bells were in place and that the sigils that Simon had marked in clear paint were unbroken.

Vic rode with extra caution. If the troll suspected that he was about to be challenged or constrained, he was likely to strike first. Vic and Simon wore protection, but the people around them were vulnerable to a powerful supernatural creature capable of creating illusions and using great strength.

Then again, if the troll overplayed his magic in plain view, it might attract too much attention. Vic hoped that meant that throwing cars around and breaking overpasses were out. That still left plenty of dangerous possibilities, like collapsing walls.

In the short drive between the bungalow and the office, the tow hitch broke on the SUV in front of Vic, setting a lawn equipment trailer loose, fishtailing across the lane.

Swearing under his breath, Vic swerved, narrowly avoiding the flatbed as well as oncoming traffic.

He pulled off to the side of the street a block later to catch his breath and still his hammering heart. The hapless SUV driver was claiming loudly to anyone who would listen that he had a chain and a padlock on the hitch that had somehow vanished.

Vic didn't doubt him and chalked the incident up to another warning from the troll.

When his nerves steadied, Vic scanned the parking lot at the station before dismounting from his bike but didn't see anyone loitering. He called Simon, who reacted immediately to something he must have heard in Vic's voice.

"What's wrong?" Simon sounded ready to drive over that very second.

"I'm okay." Vic cut to the chase. "But I think the troll sent another message." He told Simon about the incident and waited while Simon worked through his vocabulary of swear words.

"But you're safe?" Simon asked, and Vic understood his need for reassurance.

"The bike and I are just fine. Not even a scratch. I feel bad for the SUV guy, but he's never going to be able to explain a troll to his insurance company."

"I'm not sure how to ward us when we are in open territory," Simon admitted. "I'll call Gabriella and see if she has any ideas. Please—don't leave the office unless you have to, and be careful. I love you."

"I will. You, too. Love you."

When he stepped inside, Ross grabbed him before he had even finished pouring his coffee.

"I'll take your cup into the office. You've got someone waiting for you," Ross told him.

"Samuels?"

"Pretty sure it's his witchy girlfriend, Maret. I guess she decided to join the team. She's in the conference room. Already offered coffee."

"Thanks." Vic headed to join her.

Vic snuck a glance on the security camera board to get a look at his visitor before entering the room. The only description that fit was motorcycle goth. Maret looked to be in her early thirties, somewhat younger than Samuels, with dark hair tinted magenta toward the ends. Slender and tall, she wore a fringed black leather biker jacket, black jeans, and real-deal short leather boots that weren't a fashion statement.

He opened the door and tried to look like a safe contact. "Ms. Maret? I'm Detective D'amato." Vic knew from Simon that the names witches used in public were not their real names, a way to protect themselves from those who would try to gain power over them.

Maret looked up. "Detective. Thank you for seeing me. Chad spoke well of you." Her raspy voice suggested she shared her partner's fondness for cigarettes, and she smelled of menthol and verbena.

Vic moved to sit down across from her. "He spoke highly of you too. Thank you for coming to the station. How can I help?"

Up close, Vic revised his guestimate to be late thirties. She had a protective tattoo on the side of her neck, and more ink peeked from the neckline of her shirt. A Helm of Awe circle covered the back of her right hand, with an additional Norse rune on the top of each finger. On her left hand, the symbol of the goddess overlay a pentacle within a circle.

Rings of braded silver adorned her hands, which had long nails painted midnight purple. Maret wore several silver charms on chains around her neck, and Vic recognized the designs as ones Simon often inscribed. By all the measures Vic knew to look for, Maret seemed legit.

"Chad told me that the creature the club made their deal with isn't a demon, it's a troll, and that you know people who can bind it," she replied, skeptical and challenging.

"That's right. I don't have magic, but my husband and his friends do. He's pulling together a coalition of people from different magical traditions to work the incantation that originally created the lighthouses' protection. That can't destroy the troll, but it should limit the harm he can do." Vic didn't bat an eye, which seemed to surprise her.

Maret glanced at the ring on Vic's left hand and then gave him a measured look. "Magic and gay cops. What's the world coming to?"

Despite Maret's attitude, Vic liked her and suspected that at least some of her confrontational approach was defensive.

"Samuels said you head up the club's coven and might be interested in helping stop the troll. I've already mentioned you to Simon, who is gathering the team, and he said you and yours would be welcome." Vic held his breath, unsure whether Maret had come to scoff or was open to joining the effort.

"What would we have to do?" Maret's body language signaled

mistrust. Vic didn't blame her. Cops weren't usually in the habit of recruiting witches. He considered it to be a minor miracle she had even shown up to hear him out.

"A core group is going to North Island to work the incantation that created the protections over a hundred years ago. The spells gradually lost power when there stopped being live-in lighthouse keepers to renew the wardings. This should restore the protections, which limits the troll—among other things."

"Visitors aren't allowed on North Island," Maret challenged.

"Simon's got connections," Vic replied. "While he and the core group are doing that, any other witches, wiccans, root workers, and folks who want to lend their power to the effort are gathering at his store on the boardwalk. The club has agreed to protect that location, as well as heading off trouble around the homeless shelters, where the troll has been snacking between offerings."

"Yeah, he told me. Can't say I was thrilled that he agreed, but he does as he pleases." She shrugged. "Can you drop any names of these witchy types? Maybe I've heard of them."

Vic met her gaze, knowing that she was testing both his knowledge and the legitimacy of the effort. "Miss Eppie, a local root worker. Gabriella Hernandez, who owns the botanica. Their friends with abilities. The retired nuns from St. Cyprian's. And from Charleston, the St. Expeditus Society, and a witch named Rowan."

Maret raised an eyebrow and dropped the attitude. "Holy shit. They're the real deal. How the fuck—"

"Simon's the real deal too," Vic replied. "They're his network. We've worked together before."

Maret tapped her long nails on the table. "You know, I thought I'd come here and bust your chops about fake magic and feeding the club a line of bullshit. But damned if you actually know what the hell you're talking about. Good on you. This might work—and your folks might live through it."

"That's the plan." Vic was careful not to let anything Maret said get under his skin. Despite her skepticism, he sensed she had real power and hoped she would agree to help.

"Chad told me about the club being the muscle," Maret added. "They'd better not be cannon fodder."

Vic shook his head. "No, ma'am. Simon plans to provide protective amulets to everyone who wants one, as well as setting up their area with wardings to keep the troll at a distance. He's hoping there's no confrontation and that the creature focuses on the witches at the lighthouse. The club is acting as security in case the troll can manipulate humans to do its bidding and attack. Basic crowd control."

Maret didn't respond immediately, but her posture eased, and Vic sensed that his answers surprised her. If she wasn't exactly pleased, at least she hadn't gotten angry.

"What's the catch? I get Chad thinks the club owes you one for looking into Carter's death. But what about my folks? What do we owe you?"

"Nothing." Vic tried not to sound impatient. "We all get to live troll-free as long as the protections and wardings are replenished. Just a bunch of people with special abilities stopping a common threat."

"Jesus, you make it sound like you're assembling a team of comic book superheroes." Maret rolled her eyes. Vic got the insight that she was enjoying sparring with him and that if she hadn't decided to join them, she'd have already left. "We don't have to wear matching Spandex super suits, do we? Because I have standards."

Vic stifled a smile. "No matching outfits aside from your club jackets. I promise."

Maret gave a sharp nod. "All right then. You've got some witches on your side—this time. Where do you need us and when?"

"Is there a way I can contact you? Simon is firming up those details. There's a lot going on behind the scenes to pull this together."

"You have Chad's number?" Vic shook his head. She read out the digits. "Call Chad. He knows how to reach me, and I'll call you back."

Vic understood her caution. She probably had plenty of bad

experiences with cops. He could work around that. "It'll be in the next day or two, so stay close."

"Sounds like it's going to be one hell of an adventure." Maret gave a cocky smile. "Nice talking with you, Detective."

At that, she got up and walked out as if daring him to detain her. Vic understood why she and Samuels were a pair. They suited each other, both full of piss and vinegar.

Vic headed back to his office and his now-cold coffee.

"Well?" Ross asked.

"We've got ourselves a coven of motorcycle witches." Vic guzzled the coffee and refilled the cup, pausing to savor the smell of the warm brew.

"Congratulations?"

Vic shrugged. "Simon and the others are messing around with primordial energies between the troll and the natural power wellspring that the lighthouses feed into. It's a big deal to try to use magic to harness those forces. Maybe a little hubris, even. I'm in favor of anything that helps tip the scales in their favor."

Vic did his best to project confidence, and the addition of the coven was a definite win, but he couldn't shake his worry. He remembered stories his grandmother used to tell about the ancient heroes daring to try to bend the gods to their will or take control of power never meant for mortals to wield. Those stories rarely went well, and the victories were hard won.

This time around, Vic sincerely hoped the old myths were wrong.

9

SIMON

"So that's North Island," Simon said to Father Anne as their boat neared the destination. "I never thought I'd set foot there."

"It must have been a cool place to live back in the day," she replied.

The Georgetown Lighthouse, unmanned for decades, stood tall above the trees. The now-shabby keeper's house and several storage buildings remained, as well as a long pier used only by the Coast Guard for maintenance.

"I understand cutting costs, but there are times when I wouldn't mind running a lighthouse and not dealing with the rest of the world," Simon confessed.

Their chartered boat rode out the waves, forcing Simon to hold onto the railing. Cool spray hit their faces and wet their hair.

"You mean like the days when you go up against an ancient monster?" Father Anne teased, despite the danger of their mission.

"Among others."

"Glad we have someone on the inside to get us access," Father Anne said. "I hate to think what the media would do with a collection of witches and psychics getting arrested just as they're about to do an occult ritual before Halloween."

Simon shuddered, something that had nothing to do with the cold sea air. "Yeah, that would be bad."

He had gotten a call from Steven Hardin, the Navigation Aides Officer for the Georgetown Coast Guard office. Teag somehow tracked the man down and explained the situation.

Hardin had just returned to duty after a serious illness and knew the wardings needed to be strengthened. Once he found out about the effort Simon had put together, the officer had thrown his full support behind them, clearing the way for them to have access, privacy, and assurance that they would not be charged with trespassing. Hardin also arranged for a chartered boat to take them to and from North Island and volunteered to go along, together with the person he was training as his successor.

Simon promised not to leave any evidence of their presence or post any photos and agreed to share the incantation so Hardin could help maintain the protections in the future.

Now a protected wilderness, North Island no longer had any human inhabitants. Long ago, wealthy planters built summer homes and lodges there, but that ended after the Civil War. Since then, the land had become a nature preserve and home to the lighthouse. Simon wondered if any of the people who once lived there sensed the power of the land.

"Can you feel it?" Father Anne asked, and Simon nodded, knowing she meant the island's connection to the larger genius loci that ran along the coast, dotted by the other lighthouses.

"Yeah. There's a ripple of ancient energy just under the surface. Faint until you know what to look for, and then it's unmistakable." Sometimes it amazed him how many things people without supernatural abilities were blithely unaware of in their surroundings.

Out here on the water, Simon sensed the raw energies around them, both from magic and the powerful ocean current.

Everyone in their group wore protective charms and carried an inscribed demon bell. Simon counted on the amulets to help hold off the troll, but he didn't expect them to keep the creature away completely.

"You doing okay?" Vic sidled up beside Simon.

"I'm antsy. I can't tell whether it's just knowing what we're planning to do or being this close to part of the genius loci."

"Think the troll will show up?"

Simon nodded. "At some point. When he finally feels threatened. He's gotten used to doing as he pleased all those years when the guardians were gone and the protections weakened. He's not going to like getting brought to heel again."

His phone chimed, and Simon checked his messages. "The teams in North Carolina are heading to their lighthouses. Once we're all in place, we can start the ritual."

The boat docked, and they scrambled out. Vic, Simon, and Hardin helped the passengers as the captain tied up at the pier.

"Be careful," the captain warned. "No telling what's in those woods. I'll be waiting when you come back."

Simon and the others hefted their packs, filled with the materials they would need to hallow the lighthouse and strengthen its connection to the web of energy that protected the coast.

Each of the teams heading for the other lighthouses carried the same equipment, charms, bells, and copies of the incantation. Simon had checked in with the witch teams to make sure the Low Rangers showed up as promised for security, and Vic double-checked with the homeless shelters. Everyone was in place.

Simon lifted his face to the wind. The ancient power of the island made his skin itch and pulsed in time with his heartbeat. He wondered about the keepers and their families who had tended the light for decades and whether they were attuned to the resonance from the beginning or grew more so over their residency.

To what extent did the lighthouses choose their keepers? I can't imagine that someone who wasn't in sync would last long. Have the lights missed their guardians? Does the nexus have the sentience to feel abandoned?

Despite no one living on the island, it wasn't completely overgrown, and the dock was solid, suggesting that the Coast Guard kept the area around the lighthouse cleared and did routine maintenance on the pier.

Hardin led the way since he had been to the lighthouse before in an official capacity with the Coast Guard. Dan, his trainee, followed a few steps behind. Father Anne and her assistant, Beth, came next. Father Anne looked wary, and both she and Beth carried an iron ankh, a protective symbol that was as ancient as the creature they hoped to dispel.

Gabriella brought a duffel bag of the herbs and powders needed to paint the sigils and re-hallow the tower and the area around it. Miss Eppie carried a small satchel with the materials needed for her magical tradition. Sister Cecilia, the retired nun from St. Cyprian who Mrs. Ames had recruited, wore a necklace of a bishop's crozier —one of the saint's many icons—along with the amulets the others carried.

Simon and Vic brought up the rear. Simon's messenger bag held additional charms and bells, and a paper copy of the lighthouse keeper's incantation as backup to the digital version on his phone.

"You picking up on anything out there?" Simon wondered how the vibes seemed to Vic, whose strong intuition often seemed just a half-step distant from psychic ability.

"I haven't spotted the troll—although since he can shapeshift, I'm not sure what I'm looking for," Vic grumbled. He carried his gun in hand, a personal weapon, not his police service piece. "But I feel like we're being watched."

"So do I." Simon scanned the forest that verged on the cleared area around the tower.

"The whole island makes me twitchy," Vic added. "I'll be glad when we're done."

His instincts, even if they don't have psychic roots, are spot on as usual, Simon thought.

"Welcome to the Georgetown Lighthouse," Hardin told them when they reached the base of the tower. "We don't have clearance to go up in the tower, but fortunately, I don't think we'll need it. The ritual that has passed down from my predecessors is all done here at the bottom."

Simon nodded. "That matches what's in the version of the incantation I have as well." He and Hardin had already met to work out any differences between the older version of the ritual that Simon had from the long-ago keeper and Simon's more recent version. Simon had also compared notes with Father Anne to weave in anything found in the St. Expeditus archive.

They agreed that the individual keepers' spells were more powerful since they set the wardings while Hardin's version merely maintained what was already wrought. Steven had quickly agreed to cede doing the working to Father Anne.

Eager to get in and out before the troll showed up, everyone set about preparing for the ritual. Sister Cecilia and Father Anne began to paint protective symbols along the base of the tower in a substance made with consecrated and magical ingredients that faded to translucent when dry.

Gabriella set up a workspace with candles and a small brazier so she could invoke her wardings using mixtures and tinctures from plants to ward away evil and offer protection. Miss Eppie circled the lighthouse, burying small bags of goofer dust and graveyard dirt around the base. She added more invisible symbols to the inscriptions on the tower and made another circle burning a bundle of sage as she chanted.

Simon's earpiece kept him in touch with the rest of the witchy crews and the people gathered at the shop. One by one, the teams at the lighthouses reported in, ready to begin their incantations.

"Everyone's here," Pete told him, "including your Skeleton Crew and a couple of people who said they're descendants of the lighthouse keepers. We're packed to the gills, and the power is off the charts. I mean, *I* can feel it and I don't have the ability. It's practically making my hair stand on end."

"Did the coven show?"

"Yeah. They're getting along great with everyone. Don't get me wrong—everybody is taking the protective piece seriously. They've all set out their cards, charms, dice, or whatever they use, and they'll be ready to go right on time. It's like the most off-the-chain Halloween party ever," Pete added. "I hope you don't mind, but I ordered sub sandwich platters, sodas, and cookies since you always need to eat after you do a big effort."

Simon smiled at Pete's thoughtfulness and attention to detail. "That's great. Just give me the receipt, and I'll reimburse you. Did the bikers show up?"

"If you mean the six really big guys in leather lined up outside the shop, I think this is the safest we've ever been," Pete replied.

"Good. I'll let you know when we finish, but I'm going silent now so we can do the incantation," Simon reminded him.

"Good luck and be careful," Pete said. "Talk to you after."

Simon checked his newest text message and looked to Vic. "The North Carolina covens have activated, and they've supercharged the seven-pointed star. Maret's coven showed, the bikers are on duty, the store is full of witches, Pete is feeding them, and it's turned into a house party with magic."

"Why do we always miss the fun stuff?" Vic said in a dry tone. He grew serious and laid a hand on Simon's arm. "Remember what I told you. Back off and let the others fill in if it gets too much. Saving the world is important, but I want you in it." He fixed Simon with a look.

Simon took his hand. "I'll be careful. Saving the world matters, but I want to be with you." He understood Vic's caution and hoped he could keep his promise.

Father Anne joined them. "Gabriella and Miss Eppie are ready. Sister Cecilia is also finished. If you've done what you need to do, I think it's show time."

"Let's go."

Vic stood on guard, gun in hand, watching the forest. Father Anne, Simon, and Hardin stood together to speak the incantation, and the others formed a circle around them and Gabriella's candlelit workspace. Their updated version combined the best features of several variations since no one had the original text.

Hardin's assistant Dan joined Vic, standing where he could help keep watch and also witness the ritual.

Simon closed his eyes and sent out a silent summons to the ghosts of the Georgetown Lighthouse. He felt their presence flutter and grow stronger. *"Ghosts and guardians of North Island! Lend us your help to replace the wardings and keep the creature at bay."*

Spirits grew closer. Some he guessed to be the ghosts of the lighthouse keepers, while others were wives and children. A few of the revenants looked like ship captains, and Simon wondered if his call raised them from the deep.

"The power has faded. We were left alone," the ghosts accused.

"We're here to fix that. We'll raise the protections and make sure they stay renewed."

"The dangerous thing we kept at bay has gotten stronger," the spirits howled.

"Strengthening the wardings should bind the troll again. Help us."

The air grew colder, the sky darkened, and the wind picked up as the chant continued. The sea had been calm when they headed for the island, but now whitecaps rose, and waves pounded against the shore.

The troll could choose any of the lighthouses to strike, but Simon had to trust his gut that it would be drawn to protect its most powerful sources—the two strongest lighthouses.

"I'm going to cast off and go out a ways, or the boat will slam into the pier," the captain said on the frequency for Simon's earpiece. "I'll check back every half hour to come pick you up."

Without the boat, they were stranded on the island with the ghosts, the fluctuating energy of the magic—and possibly the troll. Simon tried to push that from his mind and focus on sending his energy into the spell.

He staggered when he felt the power of their ritual connect with the weak pulse of what remained of the old protections. For just a second, the invisible sigils on the tower walls lit up like flame. The warded circle where they stood glowed, and a translucent, shimmering dome of power rose over them.

Simon felt tendrils of energy expand like vines from inside the warded circle toward the tall, white tower, twining their way up the old brick walls. A flicker of light drew Simon's attention, Sister Petroula's ghost joined them, standing next to Sister Cecilia, helping with the chant.

The power of their magic rose like the tide, flowing toward the lighthouse. He recited the old words, feeling them draw from his power.

I'm glad I didn't try this alone. I'm not sure one person has enough energy to survive raising such strong protections. The spell might have taken everything I had.

Simon heard a commotion from the forest and sensed the ghosts' sudden agitation, but he couldn't spare it his attention. Not yet. Faltering now would mean failure and could be disastrous.

He felt the hair on the backs of his arms rise and knew they were no longer the only ones present on the island.

Simon had memorized the words of power. He finally dared to glance away from the page in front of him and caught his breath, only hesitating for a second as he continued to recite the words.

A tall man with the build of a professional bodybuilder— bronzed skin, broad shoulders, thick muscles, and large fists—strode toward them. His wild mane of dark hair framed plain features, and his eyes blazed golden with fury. He looked more like a warrior than the gnarled figures from fairytales and pop culture.

And here's the troll—right on time.

"Stay inside the circle, no matter what happens!" Simon was glad the boat captain had left and wasn't at risk. "That's the troll!"

Vic and Dan opened fire, hitting squarely, center mass. The troll staggered, then kept coming, barely seeming to register the shots.

He swatted away the next round of bullets—aimed for his head —like mosquitos.

The troll roared and ran at them, although he kept his distance from the lighthouse itself as if the bricks were still infused with a century of fading magic. He smelled like the wet leaves and rotting plants of the forest floor.

They fired again, and he staggered but did not fall. Inside the dome, their protections kept them safe from the troll's psychic and physical attacks, but maintaining the scrim required constant atten- tion and the addition of power. It couldn't be kept going for long without siphoning away energy needed for the fight or without harming the one casting the magic.

"Salt infused with the protections of the guardian energy will help keep him away from the lighthouse," Simon yelled above the tide.

"We'll handle Mr. Fugly," Vic said. "Do your magic stuff so we can go home and get dry."

Vic and Dan had brought a varied arsenal with them, including bullets etched with runes, shotgun shells filled with iron and silver filings, and a net infused with silver strands and soaked in colloidal silver. They didn't expect that any of the weapons would kill the troll; they just needed to weaken him long enough to do the binding.

"Time to rock and roll," Vic shouted with a glance to Dan to ensure they were in sync.

Simon had no idea how near the troll needed to be to work his magic, but Vic and Dan kept up suppressing fire to keep the being from getting close. All around him, the witches prepared for their spellwork, lighting candles and combining dried plants and other materials needed for the casting.

"He's in range," Vic told Dan. "Fire!"

The net launcher sent out a weighted web of steel with a coating of iron and silver that hit the troll with enough force to knock him to the ground.

"He's down!" Dan shouted.

The troll roared again, a near-deafening howl that rippled across the ground and was felt through the soles of their shoes. He flailed to free himself. The net was large enough that it folded around the creature, making it difficult to find the edges and get free. He hissed and shrieked, angry and clearly uncomfortable from the net's materials.

"Uh-oh." As Vic spoke, the troll struggled to his feet and banged its huge fists against the earth. The metal net cut into the troll's bronzed flesh, and the corrosive substances burned a lattice pattern, but the immortal entity kept moving. He punched at the net and then screamed as he hooked strong fingers through the weave trying to rip it apart.

"I don't know how long that will hold," Dan yelled.

Simon couldn't pause his part in the incantation to shout instructions. Instead, he sent an urgent psychic plea to the ghosts.

"Please keep the troll back until we finish. If he gets through the dome, we'll die."

The temperature dropped, freezing the spray from the waves where it fell on the ground. The ghosts who had followed them and the spirits of the lighthouse slowly faded into view, shadowy at first and then more substantial. Sister Petroula rallied the revenants, and they rushed forward, surrounding the troll.

Disoriented by the ghostly reinforcements, the troll thrashed, striking out blindly at targets that could become insubstantial and then grow solid to land a blow.

"Thank you. Keep it up. We'll be as quick as we can," Simon sent to the ghosts.

Several spells wove a similar, invisible net of protection, and Simon hoped it was even stronger than the original. Fortunately, although witches of different traditions and abilities lent their skill and energy to this new foundational binding, maintaining the power of the incantation was a much simpler ritual for Hardin and his successors.

"Shit—he's out of the net," Vic yelled as the troll shredded the last strands. The creature bled where the metal had cut into his skin, and welts rose where the silver and iron touched him.

The ghosts surrounded the troll, harrying him and withdrawing, coming at him from all directions. That deterred him for a short time until he let out a rage-filled screech. Then he made a sweeping motion with his hands that made the ghosts vanish.

Shit. Did he destroy the ghosts or send them somewhere else? Or just drain them so they can't attack anymore? Simon didn't have time to think about the possibilities, but he hoped the ghosts had not been banished forever.

The troll shrieked again and barreled toward the dome.

"Incoming!" Dan warned.

Simon looked at the others inside the dome. The binding spells took energy and focus, as did maintaining the scrim that kept the troll at bay. Exhaustion numbed him, and his head pounded. From the expressions of pain and concentration on his companions' faces, he suspected that the working was taking a toll, draining their energy and taxing both magic and life force.

We can't stop before it's finished. If the incomplete spells don't kill us, the troll will.

The possibility of being seriously injured or dying loomed larger and more likely than before.

We need to protect civilians and stop the tribute, but I don't want to die. Being a hero isn't worth leaving Vic. This wasn't supposed to be death magic.

The troll rebounded from the invisible force field, but it didn't seem to hurt him. He backed up, screamed once more, and threw himself against the scrim, coming back immediately for another hit as soon as he bounced away.

Why doesn't the troll run away? Maybe he can't.

Maybe he's bound to the land, just like the power is bound to the Wellspring.

Simon saw the effort keeping the barrier up cost the witches. He knew that the incantation and major spell still wasn't quite complete.

We may run out of time. That would be really bad for everyone.

The warding thinned, strained to its limits. A crafty look came into the troll's eyes, and he muttered something in a guttural voice.

"I will destroy you all," the troll growled.

Simon screamed in pain and wrapped his arms around his midsection, biting out the words to the spell even as he felt like his insides were on fire.

Trolls can do pain spells. Maybe it never bothered to try before, or the barrier is too thin to stop him.

One by one, the other witches staggered, doing their best to read out the rest of the spells despite barely keeping their feet.

Vic and Dan started shooting again, but the troll seemed to have figured out they couldn't kill him. The only thing at this point keeping him from wading into their group and ripping heads from bodies was the thin, fragile circle of salt, iron, and silver on the ground.

"Keep going. We've got to finish!" Simon shouted between

gritted teeth. The dome glitched, waning briefly and then waxing, and he knew they were running out of time.

Simon saw Vic shoot him a glance and knew he was worried that Simon would burn himself out. He tried to give him a reassuring look but wasn't entirely sure he could keep his promise given the cost of failure.

Sister Cecilia edged forward. Simon caught at her arm, fearing she didn't realize how close to the barrier she had gotten. She fixed him with a resolute look.

"I can buy you time—and *my* time is nearly done." She shook off his hand and stepped over the salt line—and through the barrier.

Simon's eyes widened, and he gasped, expecting the troll to tear the petite nun apart. Her lips were already moving with a curse as she crossed the perimeter, and whatever magic she wielded forced the troll back several feet. She alternated between English and Italian, hurling dark spells that ringed the creature with flames and covered its skin with boils.

We're nearly to the end. Please don't get killed.

Vic and Dan kept up their barrage, probably hoping that if Sister Cecilia's magic weakened the troll their weapons might have more impact.

The troll's supernatural healing couldn't keep up with the attack, leaving him bleeding from ragged wounds that would have felled anything natural. Fury and hatred blazed in his eyes, and Simon knew the creature would fight until too incapacitated to strike back.

We're in the home stretch. We've just got to hang in to the end.

The ghosts had returned, swarming around the troll and clawing at his arms and back. There were more spirits now, and Simon glimpsed what he guessed were ghosts of the escaped slaves. Their assault slowed the troll from returning to the warded line, but Simon knew they wouldn't be able to hold him off for long.

Sister Cecilia cast a look over her shoulder, and Simon knew it meant goodbye.

No! He cried out wordlessly since he couldn't stop the chant.

The nun threw her arms wide, ran into the troll's space, and embraced the creature as she spoke a word of power and flames engulfed them both.

"*Audios nos!*" Simon and the others chanted loudly, their voices rising as one.

The troll vanished.

The creature left behind a burned place on the sand, the melted remnants of the net, and the charred body of Sister Cecilia among dozens of bullets and shell casings.

Simon managed to stay on his feet, although he swayed and stumbled. Vic was beside him in seconds, helping him stay upright. Father Anne had paled but remained strong enough to wave away assistance. The younger witches seemed less affected but still looked exhausted. Gabriella and Miss Eppie nodded to Simon to indicate that they were okay, although he thought they looked peaked.

They all looked stunned anguished at Sister Cecilia's sacrifice. Gabriella and Miss Eppie spoke a blessing.

Simon felt the loss like a knife. *It's my fault she came with us. She deserved to live out her life in peace.*

"She knew it was dangerous when she insisted on coming," Vic said quietly, guessing Simon's thoughts.

"I could have refused to bring her."

"That wasn't your choice to make," Vic pointed out. "She lived a life of service. This was important enough to her to make a hard choice. She died a hero. You're not to blame."

Simon appreciated his words but knew it would take a long time to accept that.

"Are you hurt? Do you need a doctor—or a witch doctor?" Vic gave Simon a no-bullshit stare.

Simon ran a quick internal inventory and shook his head. "I think I'm okay. Not bleeding. The pain went away when the troll burned. I'm just spent from doing the spell. We all are."

Dan and the ghosts remained on guard in case the troll reappeared. Vic went to the cooler the boat captain left for them and returned with juice and candy bars for all the spellcasters to help them replenish their energy.

From the look on Vic's face and the grim set of his mouth, Simon felt certain his husband would be adding some vodka to his orange juice as soon as they got home.

"Is that it? Will the troll stay away now?" Dan asked.

Simon sipped the drink and shook his head. "Not forever—not without keeping the wardings replenished. The creature is immortal. We're just putting up a magical barbed wire fence around this area. There's nothing to stop the troll from causing problems with livestock or wild animals, but the binding should stop him from killing people."

"The St. Expeditus Society will work with Hardin's folks to maintain the wardings," Father Anne confirmed, and Hardin nodded.

"We're here to help any time you need us," Gabriella added, and Miss Eppie agreed.

Simon called the store. Pete answered on the first ring.

"Is it done? Because everyone here looks tuckered out," Pete blurted before Simon could even ask.

"Yes. The protections have been re-established, and we have new guardians in place to keep the spells strong," Simon told him. "Is everyone there okay?"

"A couple of people nearly fainted, and we've got folks with bad headaches, but there's no blood, and no one seems badly hurt," Pete said. "I've been passing out ibuprofen like candy and making sure everyone got plenty of carbs and sugar to help recover."

"Great. That's exactly what they need. Try not to let anyone leave until they're steady on their feet."

"I can't promise that the witches will listen to me, but I'll do my best," Pete promised. "Are you okay?"

Simon gave a grim chuckle. "The last time I felt like this was after a weekend bender in college, but I'll survive."

"Don't worry about the shop. Stay home and get better. I'll keep the lights on," Pete replied.

"Thanks. Call if anything strange happens."

"Strange for us?" Pete laughed. "That would have to be pretty weird."

"Finish your drink," Vic ordered when Simon ended the call. Simon downed the rest and handed back the can.

"It's going to take a moment to hit my system, but I don't think there's any damage. Although I might sleep for three days straight." Simon turned his attention to the ghosts, who now included Sister Cecilia among them.

"I'm so sorry." He lent the ghosts what energy he could spare so the others could see and hear.

"Don't be," she replied. "I've lived a long, full life. By binding the troll once more, many more people will be saved. It was a worthy trade. We can help the spirits of the troll's victims move on if they haven't already. And I will be honored to take my place among the guardians emeritus."

Simon planned to return the anchor items that enabled travel for the ghosts that didn't remain on the island. He looked at Sister Cecilia and hesitated.

"I can be anchored at the college and here with the lighthouse," she told him. "I feel a connection to both places. I think the other spirits will help me figure it out."

"We will make sure her memory and sacrifice are honored," Father Anne said. "I'll talk to the folks at Saint Cyprian. Be at peace," she told the ghost.

Simon turned to Vic. "What do we do about Sister Cecilia's body?"

Vic stared at the charred corpse and grimaced. "I'm still working that out."

"I'll handle it."

They turned to Hardin, who had come to stand next to Dan. "This is technically my jurisdiction under the Supernatural Coast Guard. Not my first haunted lighthouse or the first mess to clean up. It helps that no one is allowed to be here. Leave it to me."

Vic opened his mouth to argue and seemed to think better of it. *Maybe he realized that he'd never be able to write a report for this,* Simon thought.

"What we just did should break the motorcycle club deal, right?" Vic cut through Simon's silence.

Simon nodded. "Yes. With the original protections back in place —and souped up as well, the troll can't continue the deal with the club or make new ones. He's bound as long as the lighthouse incantations are strong and the genius loci of the wellspring feeds the magic."

"Good to know," Vic replied.

Simon looked to the others who had come out to the island on this desperate gambit. Everyone looked tired and worn, but proud of the difficult victory they had achieved.

Hardin signaled the boat captain, and the sound of the engine made them all turn toward the dock.

"Time to go home, folks," Hardin said. "You did good. You're heroes. It won't be in the news, but I'll make sure the right people know. Thank you."

Vic linked arms with Simon under the guise of staying close, but Simon knew his partner was quietly lending him physical and emotional support.

"Pretty impressive," Vic said quietly once they were seated on the boat and headed back to the mainland. "Now it's time to get you home and into a hot shower, feed you some sugar and painkillers, and put you to bed."

Simon wanted to make a witty, suggestive comeback but only managed to squeeze Vic's hand.

Vic leaned closer so his lips brushed Simon's ear. "We can have 'saved the world' again sex in the morning. I promise."

VIC

"I never realized saving the world was so exhausting." Simon tried for a lighthearted quip but sounded bone-weary.

"We're alive. We're tired, but no one's bleeding. And yeah, we stopped the monster. That's a big win." Vic and Simon stumbled into the blue bungalow close to midnight, utterly spent.

Vic felt jittery from the adrenaline of the fight, and he couldn't imagine what Simon must be feeling. Spell drop, the emotional and physical letdown from working powerful magic, was real, and Vic had helped Simon recover from it on many occasions. Now, Vic worried about how drawn Simon looked on the ride home and how silent he had become.

"Come on. Let's get in the shower before we sleep. Wash off all the heebie-jeebies," Vic said in a tired attempt at humor. Simon had told him once that bathing played an important part in ritual magic, sluicing away negative energy and cleansing the body to receive new power.

"Don't know if—"

"I'll hold you up if I need to. C'mon."

Vic gently maneuvered Simon into the bathroom and stripped off his clothing, looking for injuries he might have missed. To his relief, he didn't see any blood or bruises, but he knew that with magic, psychic wounds were just as real but left no mark.

"I think I'm okay." Simon didn't slur his words, not quite, but his voice was a low, exhausted rumble.

"I'll wash you. No hanky panky—this time," Vic promised with a fond smile. "Although I'll take a rain check on that. Then we can sleep. I've already told Ross I'll be in around noon."

"Need to decorate for Halloween," Simon murmured as Vic got the water temperature right.

"Worry about that later," Vic replied to the non sequitur. "Last year it took us about two hours to set up. It'll be okay."

Vic lit a sage smudge stick in the bathroom and walked around with it to make sure the smoke reached all the corners before placing it in a safe container on the counter. He'd also grabbed the special soap Gabriella had made that combined rosemary, lemon, sea salt, and lavender, all powerful for physical and psychic cleansing.

He made sure that Simon could brace himself against the shower wall before gently soaping his body. Vic ran his hands everywhere to clean and reassure. Simon permitted it, worrisomely passive, proof of how much the night's magic had cost him.

As he washed and rinsed, Vic triaged. Simon looked pale and drawn, and eyes haggard. Vic didn't pretend to completely understand what it meant to command energies like Simon and the other witches had, but he knew the aftermath of an intense night of police work, especially one that involved a stand-off or shoot-out. The adrenaline crash afterward affected mind, body, and spirit. Vic vowed to be there every step of the way for Simon, helping him to recover.

Normally shower time turned into sex in a delicious variety of positions. Much as Vic craved the proof of life validation, he knew they were both too spent.

"Later, I'm going to show you how glad I am that we survived." Vic hoped his gravelly murmur next to Simon's ear sent shivers through his lover. "But right now, I'm going to rub you down and put you to bed."

Vic toweled Simon vigorously enough to get his blood flowing and warm him. Simon was rarely so pliable, which Vic read as proof of how much the night's work had cost.

He helped Simon into baggy sleep pants and an oversized T-shirt, then shepherded him to bed and tucked him in.

"I'm going to close down and set the locks, and then I'll be right beside you." Vic gave Simon a gentle kiss.

Moments later, when the lights were out and the house quiet, Vic slid into bed, lying close enough to throw an arm over Simon and pull them together. He told himself they were sharing body heat to warm Simon, but Vic knew he needed to feel his lover's breathing and heartbeat to reassure himself that they had survived.

That was a near thing. I could have lost him. That poor nun died. We all nearly died.

I know that risk is part of the job. And I don't mind—as long as I'm the one taking the chances, not Simon.

No use dwelling on what might have gone wrong. It didn't, and we're alive and together.

Take the win and move on.

Even so, it took Vic a while to quiet his thoughts and fall asleep, and when he did, his dreams were restless.

Hours later, Vic edged a hand down Simon's pants, coaxing his cock to firmness with gentle strokes.

"There's no hurry," he whispered as Simon ground his ass back against Vic's groin. "Just relax and enjoy."

Simon let Vic work his dick until he was hot and hard, but then he struggled to turn so they faced each other. "Together," he murmured, in that sleepy growl that Vic loved so much, bedhead and all.

Vic pushed down his briefs and closed their hands over both cocks, eased by the lube he kept close by the bed.

"That's it." Vic trailed light kisses over Simon's skin. "Just go with the feeling."

It didn't take long for them to come, and it felt to Vic like the powerful shared orgasm mingled with a release of existential terror.

After another shower, Vic made scrambled eggs and sausage

links, along with fresh coffee and cinnamon toast, grateful for the extra time to collect their wits before facing the day.

"I wonder how Batman does it," Simon mused as Vic handed him a cup of coffee made the way he liked it.

"Does what?"

"Pick up the next morning after saving the city like it was no big deal," Simon replied.

"Well, he's a billionaire, so maybe he has a full spa day to soothe jangled nerves," Vic said.

"Or Alfred drugs his coffee."

"Or that."

They wolfed down two servings each, making Vic realize again how depleted they were after the previous night's events.

"Maybe tonight we can do something normal, like put up Halloween decorations," Simon suggested.

Vic grinned. "I'd like that. Dibs on inflating the dragon!"

Simon chuckled. "Okay. I'll handle blowing up the hearse with the vampire. Everyone loves those inflatables."

Myrtle Beach at Halloween had a small-town feel. Everyone might not actually know each other, but gray skies and an early sunset made for a cozy feel. Vic loved helping Simon decorate the bungalow with purple and orange light strings, spooky skeletons and fake gravestones, and of course, the eight-foot-tall dragon with mechanical flapping wings and the life-sized hearse with a vampire in the back rising from a coffin.

This year, they planned to expand the display with additional Styrofoam tombstones and a weeping angel to have a small cemetery complete with a plastic faux-wrought iron fence, ghosts, and a large fake raven.

"Is it weird that we deal with real ghosts and monsters, and then we come home and decorate for a holiday about scary stuff?" Vic wondered aloud.

"No more than how we can still enjoy a good horror movie."

"Yeah, but they get so many of the details wrong," Vic countered.

Simon gave him a fond look. "Our decorations aren't exactly accurate."

"I wouldn't know—we've never fought a dragon." Vic fought the urge to cross himself.

"And let's hope we never do," Simon replied.

"Go back to bed," Vic told Simon after they finished breakfast, as he got ready to go to the precinct. "I'll be home for dinner."

Simon nodded. "I'm not going into the store today. Pete was quite stern about telling me to rest and that he'd reschedule the couple of bookings. It's like you two gang up on me," he joked tiredly.

"We do, but it's in your best interest," Vic assured him before giving him a kiss. "If you need me, call. I suspect I'll be drowning in paperwork."

Vic decided to walk, and enjoyed the uninterrupted quiet, knowing that the day would be hectic in the aftermath of their evening activities.

"Are you okay? How's Simon—and everyone else?" Ross asked as soon as Vic showed up in their office.

"I'm tired—but worried about Simon. He's exhausted. I haven't heard from the others since last night."

"There's a fresh pot of coffee, so drink up. Cap had a meeting this morning but wants to hear what happened when he gets out," Ross said. "And I need to get the full, unredacted version."

"Are you suggesting there's more than one version?"

Ross gave him a look. "There always is—depending on who's listening."

Vic fixed his coffee and plopped into his chair. "The short version—the wardings are strengthened, the troll is bound, Simon is whole, and nearly everyone survived."

"*Nearly* everyone?"

Vic took a long sip of coffee before he replied. "Buckle up. It's a wild ride," he warned before he started his tale.

"…and then the troll vanished after Sister Cecilia burned him to death," Vic finished a while later.

"Fuck. How do we write that up?" Ross looked a bit stunned, despite having had the inside scoop on Vic and Simon's previous cases.

"*That's* what stuck with you out of the story? The fate of the coast hung in the balance, and you're worried about a report?"

"The devil's in the details," Ross pointed out.

"Lucky for us that the Supernatural Coast Guard claimed jurisdiction and is handling the cleanup. Hardin is going to work with the Sisters of St. Cyprian to honor Sister Cecilia. She didn't have any family except the cloister."

Vic provided a less detailed recap to Captain Hargrove, knowing that his boss preferred plausible deniability and would be fine with the SCG handling the aftermath.

"You know, I slept better before I knew all this mumbo-jumbo was real," Hargrove grumbled. "I liked thinking it just happened on TV."

"Where did you think the scriptwriters got their ideas?" Vic joked. "Truth is way stranger than fiction."

Hargrove held up a hand. "I don't need to know. Thanks for saving our collective asses."

"Any time."

"Is Simon okay?"

Vic nodded. "He will be. Just drained. But he took the day off to recuperate, which is progress. He used to throw himself back into work afterward until he dropped."

"You're a good team," Hargrove replied. "Glad you're on our side."

Moments after the captain left, Vic's phone buzzed. "You've got people here to see you—motorcycle folks," the officer at the front desk told them.

Vic and Ross exchanged a look. "Send them back," Vic replied.

Chad Samuels and Maret were escorted, looking defiantly uncomfortable in the police station.

"Welcome back." Vic looked at Maret. "Thanks to you and your coven again for your help."

"Glad we could lend a hand," she replied. "Simon delivered the goods. I'm grudgingly impressed—don't get used to it."

"The curse should be over for the club." Vic turned to Samuels. "The troll can't be destroyed, but the spellwork was strong enough to bind him, so the folks at the shelters should be safe again too. And your people did a great job protecting the locations. Thank you."

"Happy to help—especially if it means something stops killing my crew." Samuels extended his hand for Vic to shake. "For cops, you're okay."

Vic took the compliment as it was intended, and shook Samuels's hand. "Thanks. If you think the troll has come back, let me or Simon know. But he thinks that as long as the spell is kept strong, the troll won't be bothering anyone again."

Ross waited until their visitors had left before turning to Vic. "That's one of the most unlikely partnerships in the history of Myrtle Beach."

Vic shrugged. "Gotta start somewhere, I guess."

"Have you thought about how we are going to handle the paperwork for this case?" Ross asked.

Vic rolled his eyes. "Again you mention paperwork. No. But I'm definitely of the opinion that the less said, the better."

"Works for me."

Since there had been no official incident at the lighthouse, Vic and Ross skirted any mention of that part. No category existed for supernatural threats, let alone protecting the beach from trolls. They focused on Vic being asked by a member of the Coast Guard to do a safety check on the Georgetown light, and the report was close to the truth if extremely light on details.

The Sisters of St. Cyprian somehow finagled to have Sister Cecilia's cause of death listed as natural, which Vic supposed was true if one stretched natural to include immortal trolls.

"Hold your breath and wish me luck—I'm sending Cap the draft report." Vic pressed send.

Ross raised his hand with his fingers crossed. "Fingers crossed that he approves it. I said a prayer to the Flying Spaghetti Monster, just in case."

"I'll take any help we can get," Vic replied. "Wouldn't be the weirdest request for backup."

Ever since Vic and Simon solved their first case—a supernatural serial killer—figuring out how to handle reporting had been a challenge. Vic needed to satisfy legal requirements without including details that would subject the department to ridicule from those who did not believe in woo-woo, or implicating anyone in technically illegal behavior. That often required fudging or omitting details that were outside the norm.

Vic knocked back the rest of his cup of coffee. "After Halloween, the four of us should go out to dinner if Sheila agrees. It's been a while."

"She's been busy at work, but that should start tapering off toward the end of the year," Ross agreed. "I think we can arrange a night on the town. Are you and Simon going all out for Halloween, as usual?"

"Yeah, despite everything that's been going on, according to Simon, Halloween must be celebrated in style. It's sort of like Goth Christmas. And for him, there's the energy of Samhain as well, so he's got some special wardings and rituals for protection to do that night."

"I'm just in it for the candy." Ross popped a mint into his mouth. "Sheila and I are going out to eat and coming home after it's all over."

They looked up when Captain Hargrove walked in an hour later. Vic held his breath, seeing a printout of the report in Hargrove's hand.

"I have no doubt that you sanitized what happened to appease the mundanes," Hargrove glanced from Ross to Vic and seemed to see down to their bones. "Is there anything that isn't in here that's going to come back to bite us on the ass?"

"Steve Hardin with the Supernatural Coast Guard claimed jurisdiction," Vic reminded Hargrove. "Technically, I just did an assist."

Hargrove's eyes narrowed as he took Vic's non-answer for what it was. "I'm happy enough to let them handle it. I'd just rather not have this blow up in the news."

Vic knew the witches had made sure no one had tailed them or recorded the fight at the lighthouse.

"I have it on good authority that there won't be any leaks," Vic replied.

"There better not be," Hargrove warned.

"There won't be."

Hargrove accepted Vic's assurance with a *harrumph* but didn't argue further. "At least you've got Hardin's contact information in the report, in case anyone asks. Which they probably won't. He called me earlier. Persuasive bastard. Sounded like he had everything buttoned up."

"Look at it this way, Cap," Vic said. "We're saving time and department resources because what happened last night means no more deaths or disappearances from the Low Rangers and a significant decrease in vanishing homeless folks. No investigations or reports necessary."

"Uh-huh," Hargrove grumbled. "We'll see."

To Vic's surprise, Hargrove paused. "Thank you—unofficially. It's a big deal, even if no one else knows about it. I don't pretend to completely understand what happened—and I don't need to as long as it works. But I do recognize that there was significant risk involved and that people stepped up despite personal danger to fix a problem. So, thank you for letting the rest of us sleep well at night."

"Just doing my best to protect and serve," Vic said, although his boss's recognition meant a lot. "I'll pass that along to Simon."

"And there's a system set up to make sure the…force…behind the deaths doesn't come back?" Hargrove asked.

Vic nodded. "Yes. It's not our problem. The St. Expeditus Society is handling that—from matching guardians to lighthouses to making certain the protections are regularly reinforced."

Hargrove lifted his hand in a stop gesture. "That's all I need or want to know. Glad it's taken care of." With that, he walked out.

"Guess it's business as usual—until the next time." Ross

shrugged. "I wouldn't be disappointed if it got real boring for a while."

"I'll be very happy if the only spooky stuff I see are silly decorations and kids in costumes." Vic checked his watch. "Speaking of which—it's quitting time, and I've got a dragon to inflate."

"Knock yourself out," Ross replied. "If you have any leftover candy, bring it in tomorrow. I'll take care of it for you."

By the time Vic got home, Simon had already turned on the orange-and-purple twinkle lights and set up a small speaker on the porch to play eerie music. He had added fake cobwebs to the bushes for atmosphere. Strategically angled lights made the fake cemetery look ominous.

"I was worried you wouldn't get home in time to do the honors." Simon nodded toward the dragon and hearse, which lay in crumpled piles in their designated spots. "I already ran the extension cords."

Vic kissed him. "Thank you. Best Halloween hubby ever!" He gave Simon a quick once-over. "How are you feeling?"

"Better. I slept most of the day. It helped," Simon replied.

Vic arranged the dragon and hearse before plugging them in, letting the built-in air pumps rapidly fill the decorations. Both were lit from inside, making them stand out as the daylight faded.

"And there we go!" Vic said triumphantly as the dragon's wings slowly opened and closed. It took longer for the hearse since it was bigger, but several people paused walking their dogs to watch the inflatables take shape.

"Dinner is in the slow cooker," Simon told him. "Corned beef and cabbage with potatoes and carrots. That way we don't have to worry about it during trick-or-treat, and it'll be done by the time the festivities are over. I queued up a playlist of horror movies we haven't seen so we can do a marathon afterward."

"With snacks?" Vic looked up with a hopeful expression.

Simon made an exaggerated sigh with a fond expression. "Of course. Charcuterie board with all the trimmings and lots of good crackers."

Since Vic's introduction to the paranormal world, he discovered horror movies no longer scared him. He didn't like gore fests or movies about human psychos and sadists because they were far too real to be entertaining. But he and Simon loved poking fun at the special effects and plot holes in movies about the supernatural.

It's a strange, unexpected benefit for going up against dark magic, demons, and monsters, but I'll take it.

They dumped bags of candy into a huge bowl, ready for the onslaught.

"It's time," Simon said at six. "Bring on the madness."

For the next several hours, a parade of vampires, werewolves, ghosts, and robots came to the door, ranging from pre-schoolers to lanky college kids. Vic had to give props to the harried parents who shepherded groups of sugar-wired children while stealing a bit of grown-up camaraderie and conversation amid the madness.

"These are for the adults." Vic walked up to the parents with a bowl of better chocolate, which was gratefully raided. "I hope you have something warm and alcoholic in your future."

The night turned cool enough that Vic was happy for a sweatshirt, and he took over handing out candy to give Simon a chance to grab a jacket. The cold didn't dim the enthusiasm of the pint-sized ghosts and goblins who swarmed the steps for candy.

"I love the costumes," he told Simon as a gaggle of children walked away in search of more treats. "My brothers and I were always cowboys because it was easy."

"I'm fine with ridin' and ropin'," Simon replied with a wink that sent heat to Vic's groin. "I was 'that kid' who came up with the very nerdy original costumes. I dressed up like famous scientists for several years."

"I bet you made a cute Einstein."

Simon rolled his eyes. "Everything's relative."

Vic elbowed him. "Ha, ha. Very funny." He frowned when he realized that Simon had a far-away look in his eyes. Vic followed Simon's gaze and saw only an empty street. "Simon?"

"It's Maggie." Simon evaded the next group of kids and left them to Vic while he headed toward the corner with a piece of candy, which he added to a small pile at the edge of the sidewalk.

Kids and adults who knew the legend added to the stack over the course of the evening, and no one poached from the stash.

Vic greeted the trick-or-treaters and gushed over the costumes, but he kept an eye on Simon, who appeared to be talking to empty air. Simon let the candy fall from his hand toward the pile, and it vanished along with the rest of the candy, then he smiled and waved before returning to the house.

"Ghost?" Vic asked in between swarms of children.

"Yeah. Maggie got hit by a car back in the 1980s near that corner. As far as I can tell, she's never pulled pranks or caused problems. I don't know what she does the rest of the year because I've only ever seen her on Halloween," Simon replied. "The candy vanishes, she looks happy and fades out."

"Good to know that even ghosts like chocolate," Vic said. Simon's talent to see spirits no longer made him uncomfortable. He saw it as a way of providing solace and, sometimes, absolution. Or in Maggie's case, letting a young girl's ghost know that she wasn't alone in the Great Beyond.

The hoards of candy-seekers gradually slowed, and by the final half hour, only a few dedicated stragglers remained. Vic made sure they gave the last two kids most of the candy left because he didn't want to be tempted to eat it himself. Besides, Vic knew that Simon had a bag or two of their favorites hidden in the pantry for later.

When they finally turned off the outdoor lights and closed the door, Vic sighed in relief. They left the inflatables lit and running until the timers shut them down at midnight. He would collect them in the morning.

"Dinner smells amazing, and I'm starved." Vic locked up and followed his nose to the kitchen where Simon was plating their food.

"Grab a drink and sit—everything's ready."

Over dinner they recounted the most memorable costumes.

"Store-bought costumes are fun, but I love the ones people put together on their own," Vic said. "Some of those kids could end up being Hollywood costume designers. They've got the knack."

"My favorite was the one that looked like a dinner table with a dome over a plate—" Simon began.

"—And then an arm lifted the dome, and the kid's head was on the platter." Vic laughed. "That should have won an award."

After leftovers were put away and dishes done, Vic and Simon headed into the living room, where extra blankets were piled on the couch, ready for their marathon.

"I prepped the stuff for the charcuterie board when I made dinner, so when we're peckish, I can just bring it in." Simon plopped on the couch while Vic reached for the remote.

"And you made a horror movie playlist and queued it up." Vic turned on the television. "So bring on the thrills and chills!"

By midnight they had polished off most of the cut-up meat and cheese, along with several glasses of wine. Thoroughly stuffed, Vic and Simon snuggled close beneath the blankets as they watched heroes battle vampires, werewolves, zombies, bad witches, malicious ghosts, and a seriously malevolent possessed house.

Bad special effects made them laugh. Incorrect lore had Simon cringing and pointing out what was wrong. Vic took exception to weaponry mistakes. But the really scary parts had them glad to be safe and together.

"C'mon—let's go to bed." Vic tugged at Simon's sleeve. "I've got some ideas about ending Halloween right."

It only took minutes to clean up, turn off lights, and check the locks. By the time Vic walked into the bedroom, he found Simon waiting beneath the covers, naked.

"I want you." Simon held out his hand to Vic, who didn't hesitate. He stripped quickly and slid in beside Simon, who turned toward him, pressing close. "Whatever you want to do, I just need to feel you."

Vic answered with a kiss that started slow and deepened, growing heated. He stroked one hand through Simon's hair, holding him close and angling his head just so. Simon went along willingly.

Vic's hands slid down Simon's shoulders, then to the sexy dip at the small of his back. He firmly gripped Simon's ass and squeezed the globes, pulling him close and grinding their cocks together.

Simon tangled their legs, holding on to Vic like he was drowning. "Please," he moaned.

"Anything," Vic whispered. "I'm here. Just relax and let me take care of you."

"I put in a plug when I got home so I'd be ready for you," Simon murmured. "Just took it out and got slicked up. Want you as close as you can get."

Vic chuckled. "You weren't kidding, were you?"

"I figured that would speed things up," Simon replied with a sexy smile. "We can do long and slow later."

Vic squirted a dollop of lube into his palm and started stroking Simon's half-hard cock until it firmed in his hand, grinding against his own rigid prick. He felt Simon tremble and heard the way his breathing changed to short, sharp panting. Despite the cool night, Simon's face flushed, and he had a light sheen of sweat.

"Don't make me wait." Simon gave Vic a look so full of hunger that Vic's groin tightened. "Want to look at you while we do it."

They had tried a lot of positions and liked many of them, but Vic knew that right now, Simon wanted the comfort of having Vic top and being able to make eye contact.

Vic leaned in for another deep kiss, then pushed Simon's knees apart and back. The view of Simon on his back, laid out for him, made Vic's cock painfully hard.

"God, you're beautiful." Vic was just as besotted as on their first night together. He eased forward, testing to make sure Simon was as ready as he claimed by slipping two and then three slick fingers into his hole. He didn't want to hurt Simon and felt relieved when Simon's body accepted the intrusion without difficulty.

Vic covered him for a moment, holding his lover as close as humanly possible. He pressed kisses to Simon's neck and let his hands slide between them to tweak his nipples before he raised himself on his arms and began to move. He rocked back and forth slowly, gradually increasing speed as he felt Simon relax and lose himself in sensation.

"I love you," Vic whispered over and over. "I'm glad you're mine."

He reached down to take Simon's cock in hand, stroking him hard once more. He kept up a matching rhythm, feeling Simon gradually come apart as passion drove out stress and made him forget the aftermath of the evening.

Their climaxes hit nearly simultaneously, like riding lightning. Vic loved the way Simon shivered and clutched him tight, moaning his name. Vic wrapped his arms around Simon in the afterglow, staying joined together until Simon's breathing slowed and he relaxed, sinking into the bedding.

"Love you," Simon murmured. "Best husband ever."

"Planning to be your *only* husband ever," Vic teased gently and followed up with another kiss.

"I'm all for that." Simon sounded sleepy and sated. He tugged gently at Vic. "Time to sleep."

Vic slipped out gently and rolled to one side. "Give me a minute." He headed to the bathroom, brushed his teeth, and rinsed a warm washcloth to take back to Simon, then took his time wiping Simon down with care, making it a finishing touch of their lovemaking. Simon went to brush his teeth and came right back."

Vic lobbed the washcloth toward the bathroom door and crawled beneath the covers, spooning Simon. "Did you have a happy Halloween?" He pressed a kiss to Simon's shoulder.

"Yep. Sex with you is better than chocolate. Don't let that go to your head," Simon teased.

"Better than chocolate, huh? Then I'm all for some *hot* chocolate in the morning." Vic licked Simon's neck.

Simon reached for Vic's hand and pulled it over his heart. "Sweet dreams."

ACKNOWLEDGMENTS

Thank you so much to my editor, Jean Rabe, to my husband and writing partner, Larry N. Martin, for all his behind-the-scenes hard work, to my beta readers, and my wonderful cover artist Natania Barron. Thanks also to the Shadow Alliance and the Worlds of Morgan Brice reader street teams for their support and encouragement, plus my promotional crew and the ever-growing legion of ARC readers who help spread the word!

I couldn't do it without you! And, of course, thanks and love to my convention gang of fellow authors for making road trips and virtual cons fun.

ABOUT THE AUTHOR

Morgan Brice is the romance pen name of bestselling author Gail Z. Martin. Morgan writes urban fantasy male/male paranormal romance, with plenty of action, adventure, and supernatural thrills to go with the happily ever after.

Gail writes epic fantasy and urban fantasy, and together with co-author hubby Larry N. Martin, steampunk and comedic horror, all of which have less romance and more explosions.

On the rare occasions Morgan isn't writing, she's either reading, cooking, or spoiling two very pampered dogs.

Watch for additional new series from Morgan Brice and more books in the Witchbane, Badlands, Treasure Trail, Kings of the Mountain, Sharps & Springfield, and Fox Hollow universes coming soon!

Where to find me, and how to stay in touch

Join my Worlds of Morgan Brice Facebook Group and get in on all the behind-the-scenes fun! My free reader group is the first to see cover reveals, learn tidbits about works-in-progress, have fun with exclusive contests and giveaways, find out about in-person get-togethers, and more! It's also where I find my beta readers, ARC readers, and launch team! Come join the party! https://www.Facebook.com/groups/WorldsOfMorganBrice

Find me on the web at https://morganbrice.com. You can also find me on Pinterest (for Morgan and Gail): pinterest.com/Gzmartin, on Instagram as MorganBriceAuthor, on YouTube at https://www.youtube.com/c/GailZMartinAuthor/ on Bookbub https://www.bookbub.com/authors/morgan-brice, on TikTok @MorganBriceAuthor and now on Bluesky as @MorganBrice.

Check out the ongoing, online convention ConTinual www.facebook.com/groups/ConTinual

Support Indie Authors

When you support independent authors, you help influence what kind of books you'll see and what types of stories will be available because the authors themselves decide what to write, not a big publishing conglomerate. Independent authors are local creators supporting their families with the books they produce. Thank you for supporting independent authors and small press fiction!

Trash and Treasure

A Taste of Danger: Subparheroes

Kings of the Mountain series

Kings of the Mountain

The Christmas Spirit, a Kings of the Mountain Short Story

Sins of the Fathers

Kings of the Mountain Universe

Roustabout : Carnival of Mysteries

Sharps & Springfield Series

Peacemaker

Treasure Trail Series

Treasure Trail

Blink

Last Resort

Secrets and Ciphers, a Treasure Trail Novella

Treasure Trail Universe

Light My Way Home, a Treasure Trail Novella

Witchbane Series

Witchbane

Burn, a Witchbane Novella

Dark Rivers

Flame and Ash

Unholy

The Devil You Know

The Christmas Crunch, a Witchbane Short Story

Sandwiched, Witchbane Short Story

Ambushed, A Witchbane Novella

Midnight on the Midway: Carnival of Mysteries

Castle Magic: A Caynham Castle Collection